Them Bones

A NOVEL

J.E. Jack

Dedication

To my parents, who always supplied me with books and taught me the value of self-learning. And to my wife, Marcel, for believing in my dreams.

Table of Contents

Prologue

"It's in here somewhere," Joe thought to himself. He was searching his closet for an old baseball glove that he hadn't really used since he was a teenager, except for a few pickup games during college. He should have gotten rid of it years ago, but he liked to hold onto things, especially if they had meant something to him. His son wanted to play baseball and what better gift was there than to pass on something that he himself had treasured? The glove sure proved useful when he was in high school. He just hoped his son would appreciate it and use it as much as he did. Even though it was an old baseball glove, it was still in good shape…at least the last time he saw it, it had been. The search continued as he went through the bottom of the closet. Nope, not there. Maybe it was on the top shelf, along the back, where he couldn't see.

He reached up and blindly ran his hand along the back of the shelf and felt around. Ah… there it was, but it wasn't quite within reach. He was able to get one finger on it and move it ever so slightly. Finally, he was eventually able to wrap a couple fingers around the familiar surface of smooth, worn

1

leather and pulled it toward him. In the process of retrieving it off the top shelf, it had caught onto something else, which also came off the top shelf and fell on top of Joe before finally resting on the floor at his feet.

It was a battered, old shoebox. When Joe saw it, he knew exactly what it was and what was inside. He bent down to pick it up but instead, he put the baseball glove to the side as he sat down and pulled the box into his lap. He looked at it and he became lost in thought as his eyes gazed over the exterior of the container. Yeah, he knew what was inside and it was something that was particularly special to him. He took the top of the shoebox off and set it aside, bringing his attention back to the interior of the box. Looking inside, he reached in, his hand moving past various letters, cards and other mementos that he had received over the years. He was looking for one letter in particular and out of all of the items inside, that letter was probably the most important one to him. His fingers came to rest on the letter he was looking for and gently pulled it out. It was an old, folded up sheet of paper but one with which he took great care in unfolding; it was well-worn from being read over the years. Absentmindedly, Joe thought to himself that he really needed to do something to better preserve it. When he first received the letter, it was during a very special summer when he was kid…a summer he would never forget. He had read it almost every day, sometimes several times a day, when he had first received it. He finished unfolding it and looked over the writing. Every time he read it, he was washed over with memories and emotions. He could remember everything like it was yesterday, even though it was many years ago. When Joe finished reading the letter, his facial expression took on a distant look. It was a look that, although it appeared outward, was actually inward reflection, as he looked back on and relived the memories.

Chapter One

"READY OR NOT, HERE I COME!" Joe yelled, as he thought to himself, "I'm going to find them all." He enjoyed playing hide and go seek with all the town kids, which wasn't many. He secretly loved finding everyone and chasing them. He was relentless and was fast, which made him pretty good at doing it. It was the summer of 1992, during a rare, cool afternoon. It was a Friday and school had let out just a few weeks prior. Joe was just a couple of months shy of turning 14. He was of average height and build for that age and generally a good-looking kid. Hide and go seek was a great game for a group of kids with nothing better to do in a small town. They would have rather played baseball, but they didn't have enough kids to play and besides, they didn't even have a baseball field in town. They would have had to go to the next town over if they really wanted to play and that was a few miles away.

Joe finished counting and was on the hunt as he started looking high and low for his friends. The town—or rather, village—of Pittsburg was a small hamlet that maybe had 600 residents (but that was even a stretch) and it was surrounded by farmlands. It was a sleepy, rural community with eight cross streets, a bank, a gas station/grocery store that Mr. Brown owned, and two or three churches that tended to the different religious needs of the community. It also had a railroad track that, at one time, had been active and ran along one side of the community. The tracks were long gone by now and there hadn't been a train travel through in years. It was a small area but to Joe and his little group, it was everything they knew.

Today, they were playing near the entrance to town, behind First Baptist Church of Pittsburg; it was really the only Baptist church, though. Route 11, the only main road, went through town and on to other, more exciting places…at least that's what Joe thought. There were a couple of other roads that left town, but they went to the surrounding farms in the area, and they never had a whole lot of traffic. The main road through town was steady but it was people going somewhere else. There wasn't even a stop sign or stop light in town to slow people down. They zipped right through and Joe was sure they didn't give Pittsburg another thought once they rolled by, leaving Pittsburg in the rearview mirror. He lived here, so he knew there was nothing exciting about this town.

The woods behind the church was also where the defunct railway line was located. Since the railroad had stopped and the tracks were long gone, the only thing left was an open trail at the top of a little berm with small trestles ever so often. These served as foot bridges over the watershed ditches that flooded every time a heavy rain came through.

"Andrew! I am going to find you first!" Joe said as he got to the wood line. He had counted to 100 and started with the rambunctious spirit that one only gets when they are thirteen. He probably would find Andrew first, he thought to himself. He always found him pretty quickly because honestly, he just wasn't very good at hiding. Andrew was a couple years younger and normally, Joe probably wouldn't have hung out with him had he lived somewhere else. He was 10—just a kid. But people to hang out with were slim pickings, so the group that played together today was a group built out of necessity. No one wanted to be alone, so amends had to be made, even if Andrew was just a kid.

Not only did he have to find Andrew. There was also Frankie and Johnny who were brothers, eleven and twelve, respectively. Johnny would be the tough one to find—he always was. Last, was Matt, who was also twelve. Matt's father was the preacher at First Baptist Church of Pittsburg. Since Joe was the oldest of the group, it was his decision to play hide and go seek. Frankie had wanted to go to the convenience store and play the video arcade game *Gauntlet*, but the group didn't have a whole lot of quarters. Plus, one could only hear, "Red Dwarf needs food badly!" so many times before getting bored. In the back of his mind, though, Joe probably could have handled it a bit had he had the money to play, but his pockets were empty.

It had rained hard the night before and though the ground was dry, there were a couple areas that

7

were soft, which was great for Joe because he could see footprints in the mud facing the railroad berm and trestles, which wasn't too far ahead. When Joe got to the top of the berm, he stopped short. There were all the other kids in a group, just ahead, and looking down the berm on the other side.

"Guys! You were supposed to hide," Joe said. "I'm not counting to 100 again."

Sure, he liked chasing people but counting to 100 took time and he would only do it once, especially when no one went and hid like they were supposed to do. They all seemed startled when Joe yelled and Andrew looked back to Joe, "You gotta come take a look at this."

Andrew was a short kid with glasses that he always fiddled with. It seemed that he was always either pushing them back on his face or cleaning them...or cleaning them and pushing them back on his face. The rest of the group stood still. Brothers Frankie and Johnnie almost looked identical; people were always surprised to find that they weren't twins. They always wore ballcaps except when they were in school. Then there was Matt, who was taller than all of them, played basketball at school and was a bit on the gangly side.

"Come on guys, what could be so imp..." Joe stopped as he got up to them and saw what they were looking at. It was a small tree that was blown over in the storm from the night previous, Joe guessed, but it wasn't the tree that captured their attention. Where the tree met the ground, the roots had pulled up the dirt around it and it looked like…bones? Not pearly white bones like Joe had seen in science class, but dirty, brown bones. These bones looked like they had been there a while.

They stood transfixed for a bit, before Johnny said, "It's probably animal bones."

"Yeah, probably," Matt answered.

"I'm going to go down and take a closer look," Joe said.

"Eww…gross," Andrew said.

"Don't be a baby, Andrew," Joe replied.

"I'm not a baby, I just don't want to get close to something that's obviously dead. Yuck," Andrew said.

"Then don't. Stay here," Joe said, as he started down the other side of the berm to get closer to the overturned tree. The group reluctantly followed Joe but Andrew decided to stay at the top of the berm, giving whatever it was wide berth, "Don't touch it," He said.

Joe said, "It's probably deer bones."

No one else said anything as they got closer. Indeed, it was hard to tell what kind of bones they were. If they hadn't been looking, they might have been mistaken for roots, but it looked unnatural in a natural sort of way. They weren't connected, and they just lay there singularly together, a bit jumbled by the tree shifting the area around them, which ultimately uncovered them.

As Joe got to the bones, he looked around in the shallow pit and noticed something buried at one end. It looked like a ball but he wasn't sure. He felt compelled to find out what it was so he stepped closer, bent down, and removed the dirt to uncover whatever it was.

Andrew, still at the top of the berm, repeated, "Don't touch it!"

The other boys who had joined Joe didn't want to get closer when they saw what he was doing. Johnny warned, "Yeah, don't touch it. What if it had a disease or something? You know, I once heard about …" but trailed off when he realized no one was listening to him.

There was something that just felt "off" about everything and Frankie was getting fidgety now. "Let's go do something else… hey! Let's go get some soda. I'm thirsty anyway."

The group shuffled around a bit, then Matt agreed with Johnny. "Yeah, we can run up to Mr.

Brown's store, I always like hanging out there. It's neat to see the people come and go. And Joe, I have some extra quarters to play that game."

The mention of more quarters piqued Joe's interest in heading up to the store but he had to find out what was uncovered by the tree first. The group started to move when Joe yelled at the group. "Hold on guys! I'm almost done and then we can go. I just want to see what this is."

He uncovered the ball enough to be able to grab it and lifted it from the dirt. It felt hard and gritty. When he turned it around to look at the other side, what he saw was a human skull with a crack jaggedly running down one side. The gaping holes where eyes used to be, stared endlessly back at him. Everything in Joe's world went black.

Chapter Two

Joe woke up with a start. He was in his bedroom and he could see through the window that it was dark outside. His mom and dad were at the side of his bed, with his mom sitting in a chair and his dad standing over her shoulder.

"Oh, thank goodness! I am so glad you're okay!" his mom said. "You gave us such a scare."

His father said, "Well, you gave your mother a scare. I knew you'd be all right." He continued, "Seeing a dead body can do strange things to people."

Joe heard the words his dad said and was confused about what he heard. Dead body? He couldn't remember…Okay, it was coming back to him now. It was a nice, sunny afternoon and he was playing games with his friends in the woods. Then he remembered vividly. The dark pools for eyes that the skull had, stared at him with a piercing look that latched onto and into him like some weird connection. It was almost like a feeling of electricity that went deep inside his own soul. He couldn't explain it; in fact, just thinking about it made him feel lightheaded.

As suddenly as the memory of the experience of connection came, it was gone.

"Dead body?" Joe asked.

"Yes, honey, don't you remember? The boys came running back to get help this afternoon. The boys said you fainted, and your dad and I ran out there, found you and carried you home. Once we saw what was out there, we called Sheriff Mattson to come," his mom said.

"How are you feeling, Joe?" his dad asked.

"I'm feeling tired. Just really drained, Dad. I don't remember exactly what happened but…" Joe was trying to find words to explain but couldn't.

"It's okay son; you are okay," his dad said.

They all heard a knock on the front door. Being a small home, noises traveled throughout the house. Joe's father said, "I'll go see who it is."

He left the room and went to the door. Joe could barely hear his dad welcome the visitor inside. After a few moments, he came back to Joe's bedroom door. "Karen, the Sheriff is here and he would like a moment."

"Okay…" She got up to leave and then turned back to Joe. "It's okay son; go back to sleep. Things will be clearer in the morning."

She leaned down, kissed him on the forehead, then left the room, pulling the door to but not closing it. The light from over the kitchen table spilled down the hallway and Joe could see it create a narrow beam into his room and onto the wall. It seemed to be trying to battle the dim light coming through his window from the street light.

Joe could hear the sheriff come in and both he and his dad sat down at the kitchen table before the conversation started. Sheriff Luke Mattson was a good friend of his dad's and although he was friendly, he could be real intimidating at times. They were hunting buddies who met when Harold, his dad, first moved to town. With Harold being a military veteran and Luke being a deputy sheriff, they naturally got along and would often go shooting together. Of course, as Luke's responsibilities became more while he was rising through the ranks, especially after he was elected sheriff, they didn't recreationally shoot as much as they had in the past.

"Want some coffee, Luke? I can put on a pot," his dad asked.

"No Harold, I'm not going to take too long here." But then the Sheriff thought about what he had to do that evening in regards to returning to and organizing the crime scene. "Actually, it's going to be a long night. Would you mind? I would be grateful."

Harold started to get up, but Karen came into the room and told him to sit back down. She would take care of it.

"So, what's going on?" Harold asked.

"Well, I am going around to all the kids' houses to see if they took anything from the crime scene. I'm sure they didn't but I just wanted to cross that off the list. It also gave me a minute to return to the office to grab more supplies to take back out there with my deputies," the sheriff said.

"Well, Luke, Joe didn't take anything. We brought him home. He fainted at the sight of it," Harold said.

"Yeah, like I said, just crossing things off the list to make sure."

"What do you think happened? How long do you think them bones have been there?"

"Well, I'm not sure. We won't know one hundred percent, but the bones are small and the only thing that I can think of is that we had a missing person—well, a kid really, that went missing about 12 years ago, in 1980. A fourteen-year-old girl named Mary Teller. Never found her. We searched and searched and nothing. I hope it's not her. But I know the family would like to have closure, so I'm torn."

"Oh wow!" Harold exclaimed. "I remember something about that. We moved here shortly after—well, it was a year or so after it happened. Her father worked with me at the mine when we first moved here, before he retired. Well, we didn't work together—he was on a different shift."

"So, you think it's her? Oh dear, her poor family," Karen said.

The Teller family still lived in the town of Pittsburg, just on the outskirts. Their house was on the other side of the woods from the Baptist church where Joe and his friends had been playing when they found the bones. Mrs. Teller was actively involved at that local church, though Mr. Teller didn't do much, it seemed, after he retired. He kept to himself and rarely left the house unless it was to go grocery shopping with his wife. He wasn't unfriendly. He would wave at people he knew as they were passing by but he wasn't known for being super-friendly. Samantha, their daughter, had been eight at the time of Mary's disappearance and was now twenty and going to the local community college. Mrs. Teller never wanted to leave the town, in hopes that Mary would show back up one day but so far, she hadn't. Each passing year of not knowing what happened to Mary brought a little more despair until it had just become their norm.

About this time, the coffee was done. Karen not only poured a cup of coffee for the sheriff, but also got out one of Harold's work thermoses, filled it up and then put it on the table along with the cup.

"Here, take this thermos with you. If it's going to be the kind of night you think it will be, you are going to need it. Just bring back the thermos when you can," Karen said.

"Thanks Karen. I really appreciate that," Luke said.

Joe didn't hear much of the adults' conversation in the other room; it was sort of muffled. Anyway, he was super tired and it took energy to pay attention. No matter how interesting the conversation was about some girl who disappeared years ago, he just couldn't keep his eyes open. The sandman was working overtime and his eyes were feeling droopy and heavy.

Just as Joe was about to drift off into a deep sleep, he thought he saw something in the dark corner off his room, opposite the wall where the light from outside his window and hallway fell. He couldn't quite make it out. It looked like an outline of someone—like seeing an image through a blurry window, in that dark corner. But when he focused on it, it was gone. He had a long day and attributed whatever it was to the extreme tiredness he felt. It wasn't long before he closed his eyes and drifted back to sleep.

Joe woke up later to the smell of lavender wafting through his room. It left him with a peaceful feeling. It had to be past midnight, he thought; all the lights were off in the house. As Joe lay there in the dark, he started to become aware of a presence in his room.

"Mom?" Joe said sluggishly, as he was wiping the sleep out of his eyes. He still wasn't totally awake, but he was aware that someone was there. He reached for the small lamp that was on the small table next to his bed. He turned it on and looked around the room but didn't see anything. "Weird," he thought. He didn't feel the presence anymore, either. He got up and looked around the room; he even went to the closet and peaked in. Nope, nothing there either. "What a strange day," Joe thought to himself as he climbed back in bed. He turned off the light and again, drifted off to sleep.

Chapter Three

The sun streaming through the window woke Joe up the next morning. He could smell bacon that his mom was cooking, and he was ravenous. He realized that he hadn't eaten anything since lunch yesterday. He tore off the blanket and bounced out of bed, then headed into the kitchen.

His mom greeted him cheerfully. "Good morning, sleepyhead. You must be hungry."

"I am!" He replied as he grabbed a glass from the kitchen cabinet and then went to the refrigerator to fill it up with orange juice. He was thirsty, too. He downed it and then filled it again, before putting the carton back and then going to the kitchen table to sit down. It wasn't long before his dad joined him.

"How are you feeling today?" his dad asked.

"I feel good," Joe said.

"What are you planning on doing today?" his dad continued.

"I'm not sure," Joe replied.

"Yeah, I thought about going into town. Mr. Winters asked me if I could pick him up some feed for his horses and thought you could come help," his dad said.

"That sounds great," Joe said.

Later that morning, Joe and his father piled into the family truck. It was a two-toned truck from the mid-80s; it was dark brown with a horizontal, light brown stripe going down each side. It looked like it had been ridden hard but Joe's dad took good care of it and he liked to refer to it as "Old Faithful." That truck always started and had never given any problems except for your normal wear and tear.

As they backed out of the driveway and into the street, Joe noticed a girl on the sidewalk in front of his house, just standing there. He had always liked girls but just recently, he started to really notice them, like a blip on the radar. Whenever he was near one his age, his attention would pique and then he would get all nervous. Even though he liked the opposite sex, he always felt weird around them. This girl looked to be about his age and he thought she was very pretty. He wondered who she was. He had never seen her before. She had straight, long, dark hair and was wearing jeans and what appeared to be a two-toned "baseball sleeves" shirt. She also had on a jean jacket, which Joe thought was strange because it was summer and warm out. The girl seemed to be watching the truck but Joe couldn't really tell, because this all happened in a matter of moments, while they were on going in the opposite direction. Joe turned around to look again, but didn't see her. He thought it very strange but turned back to the front and settled in for the ride. He would have to ask around to see who she was.

Harold and Joe left the little town of Pittsburg and headed toward the bigger city of Avondale, which was about twenty miles away. Avondale wasn't that big of a city but it was much bigger than Pittsburg. It had all the essentials. For this area, Avondale seemed like the sun with all the smaller, farming communities (like Pittsburg) floating around it for stability. It was also where the area high school was located, and Joe expected to be going there in a couple of years. On the way, Joe and his dad broke into conversation. It was small talk for the most part; they talked about plans for the summer and then it drifted toward the events that happened yesterday.

"So how are you feeling about yesterday?" Harold asked.

"Okay, I guess," Joe replied, then continued, "So, it was a missing girl?"

"Oh, you heard that conversation, huh?" his dad asked.

"Yeah…I mean, yesterday was fuzzy and I was pretty out of it last night, but when I heard it was the sheriff, I wanted to hear," Joe said.

"That's what they are thinking. They don't want to confirm anything until they are absolutely, one hundred percent sure. I spoke to Luke this morning and through the evening, they excavated the area and found more items that they think will help identify the bones," Harold said.

"Just kind of sad, really," Joe said, thinking aloud, "that something like that would happen in Pittsburg. I never would have thought that would happen here."

"Indeed, son and to think, all this time, that girl was out there. It is very sad," Harold said.

A few minutes later, they pulled into the parking lot of Barnard's Feed store. It was half feed store, half hardware store. They had everything a person who made their living on a farm would need—from tools to harnesses to food, for both crops and animal agriculture. It smelled of sawdust and had been there for a zillion years, Joe thought, but in reality, it had only been there since the 1940s.

As his dad went to the back, to talk to one of the attendants about Mr. Winter's order, Joe walked around the store with nothing particularly in mind that he wanted to look at. He passed the toy shelf that had plastic barnyard animals; cowboys and Indians; as well as little, green, Army men. Even at Joe's young age, he could tell these toys weren't "modern," but he figured the store owners probably didn't know any better; truth be told, they didn't. But toys didn't really interest him much anyway; he was getting to that stage of life where toys just weren't fun anymore. He wandered over to the magazine rack and picked up the latest edition of *Field and Stream* and flipped through that. He liked the pictures of animals he would find in the magazine, as well as the advertisements for the different shotguns and rifles. He enjoyed that because his dad would take him shooting sometimes and there was nothing he enjoyed more than spending time with his dad, shooting targets.

After he was done, he put the magazine up and went to the front of the store. It wasn't crowded, though it did have its fair share of customers for a Saturday morning. This was the day when people who were farming enthusiasts would come into town to get their supplies, as they had to work a normal day job during the week. They were serious about farming but couldn't live strictly on it. Most of them farmed for additional food supply and extra income when there was a surplus. Joe didn't recognize anyone and looked out the front window of the store. It was one of those large, display-type windows so that anyone out in the parking lot could see in the store and see what was for sale. It was also good for the natural lighting that enhanced the fluorescent

lights that lit up the store. He was in the midst of turning around to go to the back to see what was holding up his dad when he noticed a figure in the parking lot, looking through the window at him. He quickly looked back and saw that it was the same girl...no it couldn't have been the same girl...but it was. It was the same girl that Joe saw out in front of his house; the same pretty girl with long, dark hair.

She was looking straight at him through the window. There was no way that she could have seen him because he wasn't at the front of the store; he was near the front, but not where someone outside could see him. He'd been at this store enough times to know what could and could not be seen at this time of day. But there was no doubt—she was looking straight at him. She was strangely out of place. She stood there without a care in the world, people moving all around her. It was as though she didn't notice them, or that they didn't notice her. The girl had a pointed look on her face, as if she was searching, and then she smiled at him. Joe just knew it—she smiled directly at him. It made Joe catch his breath and step slightly back, out of surprise and a low feeling of anxiety creeping up in his stomach. Joe wanted to get a better look and had to step around a pillar that momentarily blocked his view. When he got around to the other side, she wasn't there anymore. Joe's mind couldn't compute what had just happened. He walked quickly to the front window and looked out over the parking lot, but she wasn't anywhere to be seen. She might have ducked behind some vehicles. That was possible but she wasn't anywhere that Joe could see.

"Ready to go?"

Joe came out of his daze of looking out over the parking lot, searching, to see his dad leaving the checkout aisle.

"Sure," Joe Said.

Harold stopped short. "You okay son? You look like you've seen a ghost."

"What? No…nothing. I thought I saw something outside but it's nothing," Joe replied.

"Okay, let's get this stuff to Mr. Winters."

Mr. Winters lived on one of the many farms that surrounded Pittsburg. He was an older man that went to church with Joe's family. He was a widower who had lost his wife a couple years back. He was still strong as an ox though that ox wasn't quite as strong as it used to be. Joe's dad would help him out from time to time with things around his farm. Not all the time, but just enough; it wasn't a bother to Joe's dad and he enjoyed doing it.

After a ride through the country, they made it to Mr. Winter's farm and Joe helped his dad unload the supplies. Mr. Winters had a couple of cows and horses and he also had a nice-sized garden. Joe didn't know Mr. Winter's exact age but he figured he was in his 80s. Joe remembered Mrs. Winters and he really liked her. He was sad when she passed. She was always so sweet to him. She treated him like he was one of her grandkids, though her grandkids were already grown.

As they pulled up to the house, Mr. Winters motioned to drive over to the barn as he was heading that way. They stopped just short of the barn and Harold put the truck into park. "Okay, Joe, let's unload this stuff and get on home for lunch."

"Sure thing, Dad," Joe said.

They both got out of the truck and along with Mr. Winters, started carting the feed to the barn. As they were doing this Mr. Winters said to Joe, "News travels fast in this town, young man. With everything that happened yesterday, are you okay?"

"Yeah, I'm fine. It wasn't anything gruesome or anything like that. I'm not sure why I passed out," Joe said.

"Still, pretty amazing discovery, though," Mr. Winters said.

Joe's dad broke in, "They think it's that girl that disappeared all those years ago."

"That would make sense. She was the only person in the area that no one knows what happened to," Mr. Winters said, and then continued, "Yeah, I remember that mess. It was so sad. I really felt for her family."

Joe's dad asked, "What do you think happened to her?"

Mr. Winters looked off and his eyes went distant for a few moments, looking for old memories, and then answered, "Well, there were a lot of rumors. I think everyone was under suspicion or the target of different stories. You gotta understand, and you do, this is a small town. Something like that causes everyone to become afraid, even of their own neighbors."

"I heard all kinds of stories…from people saying it was her own family's fault for her disappearance, to Mr. Brown at the convenience store, to some drifter that came through town. I am not sure what happened. I can only speculate," Mr. Winters said.

Again, Joe's father pried, "Well, what do 'you' think?"

"I don't know. I kind of think it could have been a drifter, but I don't really remember hearing about, or seeing any during that time. Everyone really loved that little girl. She was sweet and super-friendly, from what I could tell and remember. Her teachers loved her, her neighbors…it was quite the shock."

"She went to my school?" Joe asked.

"Yup, she did," Mr. Winters said.

Joe went to Pittsburg primary school; the mascot was the Pittsburgh bulldogs. It was on par with being a small school in a small community. It serviced grades 1st to 8th, before they went to the high school over in Avondale. It only had a couple of teachers that taught multiple grades, and a gym coach. It had been bigger in the past, but as the community dwindled to modernization and young folks moving to the city and no longer getting into the family business of farming, it had downsized a lot in the past twenty years. There had been talk of shutting down the school and combining it with several other small communities to make a bigger school but so far, that hadn't happened.

"Were the teachers the same?" Joe asked.

"Yeah, Mrs. Miller, she taught there. So did Coach Dill. Mrs. Johnson, she left oh...back in the mid-80s sometime and was replaced by Mrs. Beckett," Mr. Winters said. He had a rather good memory and was well-connected in town. He knew everyone, but Joe kind of laughed at this to himself. Everyone knew everyone in this town.

It didn't take long to get everything from the store in its appropriate place and Joe and his dad said goodbye to Mr. Winters before heading home. It was not yet noon when they pulled up into the driveway of their house and went inside, but Joe still felt a little "off" and wasn't hungry. Instead of waiting for lunch, Joe asked his dad if he could go play with his friends. His dad told him that it would be okay but to stay within yelling distance if something came up.

He ran out the door with his mom yelling, "You be careful!"

Joe headed to his friend Matt's house. He was halfway down the block, lost in thought, when he smelled a strong scent of lavender. It wasn't overpowering but enough to draw him out of his thoughts. He looked up and was surprised to find that he was no longer alone. The dark-haired girl that he noticed earlier was there in front of him, just a few steps away on the sidewalk, looking at him. She wasn't there just a few moments ago; the street had been clear. She smiled at him and his world went sideways. Next thing Joe knew, he opened his eyes and realized he was on the ground. The dark-haired girl was standing over him, looking down with a look of concern on her face. "Are you okay?" she asked.

"Y…y…yeah," Joe stammered. "I don't know what happened."

She smiled, almost giggling, and said, "You took one look at me and passed out. I don't think that's ever happened to me before. I don't know if I should be flattered or scared. Do I have that effect on people?"

"Yeah...ah…no. I'm so confused," Joe said and squinted up at the girl. She held out her hand to help him up, and he took it. Her hand was cool to the touch and very soft. When he got on his feet, he brushed off the dirt and grass.

31

"Thanks for helping me up. I don't know what that was about," Joe said, indicating the ground he just got up from.

"It's okay. You've had a long couple of days," she replied.

Joe looked sharply at the girl, his mind racing. How could she know what kind of days he had been having? He had never seen this girl before and he would have remembered her. She was cute in a way that would have left him tongue-tied had he met her somewhere else.

"Who are you?" he asked.

"I'm Mary."

Chapter Four

Joe about fell over again, but this time it wasn't the sudden, black-out type experiences he had been having. It was more along the lines of a brain trying to grasp a concept that just wasn't connecting, but at a speed that was too fast for comprehension. He looked at Mary puzzledly and said, "Mary?"

"Yep, that's me!" she exclaimed exuberantly, then continued, "It's nice to finally meet you. I've been watching you the last little bit."

That little tidbit of information freaked Joe out even more, leaving him wondering what she was talking about. "What do you mean?" he asked uncertainly, but his brain was already working on a hypothesis that only she could answer.

"Do I have to spell it out for you? Okay, I know I'm dead. I just don't know how long I've been in that ground, but it feels like a while. You did something when you touched my bones. Wherever I was and whatever you did, it's the first time in a long time that I felt anything other than being cold and in a dark place. So, I'm connected to you in some way. I don't know why or how but I guess it just took your brain some time to see me, but I saw you immediately when you blacked out beside my grave."

And in Joe's mind, the worst possible hypothesis that was just confirmed—he was talking to a dead girl.

She stood there, looking at him. "Are you okay?" she asked.

It took a moment for his brain to catch up and understand what she was saying. "Yeah, I'm fine...I think," he said. "I'm just trying to process all of this," he continued.

"Oh, I'm sure. Trust me when I tell you that it was just as surprising to me. Especially when I tried talking to you before and you weren't seeing or hearing me. I thought, 'Oh, great, I am stuck following this guy around and he can't even see me.' But then I noticed that you started responding to me," she said and then smiled the most beautiful smile Joe had ever seen. "I'm glad you can see me now."

"Hey Joe!" they heard someone calling from down the street and Joe turned to see who it was. He saw that it was the brothers Frankie and Johnny, complete with matching ball caps, riding up on their bikes, looking excited to see Joe. He stepped out into the street to meet them.

"Dude, you totally passed out yesterday. Are you doing okay? We were so worried!" Johnny said breathlessly while bringing his bike to a stop in front of Joe.

"Yeah man—you totally zonked out. We had to go run for help," Frankie said.

"Yeah, I don't know what happened. I mean, I am a bit tired today but okay for the most part," Joe said. Then he remembered Mary, and continued, "Guys, I want you to meet..." He turned to introduce Mary but she was gone.

"Meet who?" Johnny asked, looking around but seeing no one.

"Are you sure you're all right?" Frankie asked.

"Yeah, I'm fine...uh...no one I guess. I don't know what I'm talking about. I guess I'm still little out of it," Joe said.

Matt and Andrew came roaring up the street on their bicycles. They weren't far behind Frankie and Johnny and were also excited to see their friend. They asked the same questions that the brothers just asked to see if Joe was okay, to which he replied the same.

"It's so good to see you," Andrew said. "Your parents came and then the sheriff and we didn't know what was going on. We thought the worst."

"You guys can't get rid of me that easily." Joe smiled, starting to feel himself again.

"We never wanted to," Matt quickly replied. He was always quick-witted and quick with a response.

"So, what happened?" Johnny asked.

"They don't know. I just passed out," Joe said.

"Did you hear? They think the bones are of a girl that lived here a long time ago," Andrew said.

"Yeah, my dad told me it's the Teller family's daughter," Matt said.

"Oh, that's right. I had forgotten about them," Andrew said. They quickly devolved into conversation about what they thought had happened or what they heard from other people about what happened the night the Teller girl disappeared. The whole time Joe was thinking to himself, "Where is Mary? Why did she just disappear on him?" But he had a feeling that he would see her again, real soon. Whatever it was that was going on, it was far from over. And if he were honest with himself, he was kind of looking forward to it. It's not every day that he got to talk to a pretty girl, even if she was dead. When he reminded himself of that, it snapped him out of his thoughts and back into the conversation the other boys were having.

"Well, I heard that it was a transient," Matt said.

"Who would be a transient here, Matt? Johnnie asked. "It's not like this town attracts people."

"Well, that was during the time that the trains came through this town. Maybe someone hopped off, killed her and then hopped on another train out of here," Matt said.

"What's a transient?" Andrew asked.

"Oh, that's a person who rides a train," Matt said matter-of-factly.

"Are you sure?" Andrew asked. "I thought it meant something like a homeless person, but I am not one hundred percent on that."

"Oh yeah—definitely," Matt said.

It wasn't long before the boys moved back up the street and headed toward the gas station, where Mr. Brown was a common fixture behind the counter. It was a small, two-pump gas station that kept the townsfolks' cars running. It was a lazy operation in that there was not enough traffic to be busy, but just enough to be steady, with maybe a car or two stopping every thirty minutes or so. The boys enjoyed hanging out there and Mr. Brown tolerated them hanging out front. They were good kids and didn't bother the customers, the few he had from time to time anyway. In fact, he was bored most days and enjoyed chatting with anyone who would talk back.

Joe walked into the store. It was a normal-looking gas station with a couple of vending machines outside, near the door. Inside, there were a few rows of things that people who were traveling might need, such as snacks, candy, canned goods, motor oil and such; then there were more drinks in a couple of glass coolers at the back of the store. It also had a couple of arcade games that the kids of the town fed countless quarters into. With Mary still in the back of his mind, lingering in his thoughts, he decided to ask Mr. Brown about her. Mr. Brown had owned the station for twenty plus years and he was always there, behind the counter. The gas station didn't do too well financially but it was enough to live on, at least for Mr. Brown.

"Hey Mr. Brown."

"Hey yourself, Joe. How's your family doing?"

"They're doing fine."

Mr. Brown must have been over sixty years old, maybe close to seventy. He had dark grey hair and thick, brown plastic-rimmed glasses that he looked through. He was slightly balding and was of thin build. He more or less shuffled along instead of walked.

"Mr. Brown, may I ask you a question?" Joe asked.

"Shoot."

"Did you know Mary Teller?"

"I did. She would come here from time to time like you boys do. Some things change but some things don't, such as bored kids in a small town. Bad business though, what happened to her. I heard they found her bones in the woods. So sad, she was such a nice girl," Mr. Brown said.

Mr. Brown got a far-off look in his eye before continuing, "It was such a strange thing to happen in this small town. Nothing like that has ever happened. We were all worried and curious as to what happened to her. But then, as time goes on, you just sort of move on until it's just a memory or forgotten."

He took his glasses off to wipe the dust off. "I am glad they found her, though. Hopefully, they will find the person who did it but really, I'm glad that her mom finally has some answers, even if they aren't great answers. At least now she knows. Why do you ask?"

"Oh, I don't know," Joe said. "She was around my age when it happened, so…curiosity? What do you think happened to her?"

"Well, Joe, I do a lot of thinking behind this counter. I have more time than I know what to do with most days. Sure, I hear all the gossip and I've heard it all but when it comes to the subject of Mary Teller, I just don't know," Mr. Brown said.

"What did she look like?" Joe asked, even though he supposedly met her. He wanted to make sure it wasn't some weird hallucination or some sort of psychological condition he was experiencing.

"From what I remember, she was liked by everyone. Had long, dark hair; blue eyes. She was a real cute girl. Very friendly. Such a shame something like that happened to her. You know, Joe, sometimes life doesn't make sense," Mr. Brown said.

"Nope, it sure doesn't, Mr. Brown," Joe thought to himself.

Chapter Five

It wasn't long after they arrived at Mr. Brown's store that Joe's stomach started grumbling and he was getting hungry. The other boys were hungry as well, so they decided to break for the afternoon with plans to hang out later, if nothing else was going on with their families. To Joe, this was fine. He was kind of looking forward to getting home alone and hopefully, Mary would appear again, and they could talk. As weird as everything was, he felt comfortable with it. He walked through the front door of his home and went directly to the kitchen, where he made himself a sandwich, then proceeded to munch away as he headed to his room. The sandwich was gone by the time he got there; he must have been hungrier than he thought to wolf it down so quickly.

With his parents outside enjoying the weather, he decided to see if what he had in mind would work. He closed his eyes, took a deep breath, shut the door, then turned around. Half of him was hoping that Mary would appear and half was hoping that she wouldn't. When he opened his eyes, there was Mary sitting, on his bed. Even though he half-expected it, it still shocked him.

"Hey Joe!" Mary said.

He just stood there and looked at her, suddenly feeling nervous. She really was a cute girl.

"What's wrong? Cat got your tongue?" she asked.

"Nothing is wrong," he replied quickly. "What happened to you earlier? You just vanished."

"Only you can see me, and you are the only one I can talk to," she said.

"How do you know that? You said before that I couldn't see you but then eventually, I did."

"Hey, this is all new to me too, but I am ninety-nine percent sure that I can only talk to you. I'm connected to you somehow." She smiled disarmingly and continued, "Which isn't a bad thing. You seem nice."

Joe flushed a little. In fact, he could even feel the blood rise in his face as it darkened a shade red. Mary started laughing. "Oh my goodness, you're blushing! I didn't know I had that effect on people."

This only made Joe blush more. Seeing that Joe was on the brink of embarrassment, Mary decided to change the conversation to give Joe some breathing room. She thought he was kind of cute, which was a weird thought that she would even think about such things, being dead and all…but she wasn't dead. She just wasn't fully present. She still had thoughts and she could still feel.

"But yeah, since I didn't want you to look like a crazy person trying to explain something no one could see, I thought it better that I just…left," she said.

"Where do you go?" Joe asked, thankful to get back on topic. He could already feel his face cooling.

"Well, I don't really leave; I just don't show myself. It's weird. I can decide to show myself or not show myself to you. I don't know how I do it. It's just like lifting my arm or wiggling my fingers…I just do it. I mean, for all you know, I could just be a figment of your imagination. Haha…I'm your imaginary friend," she said laughing, but then immediately sobered up and continued, not quite sadly but resigned. "But, I was real and alive once, and I am real now."

"So, you are like…around me all the time?" Joe said.

"Yup," she replied.

Immediately, Joe blushed again thinking of his shower and bathroom activities earlier that day. As if reading his mind, she quickly added, "Oh, don't worry. I give you privacy. I don't wanna see that!"

"Uh…thanks?!" Joe said because he honestly didn't know how to respond, then quickly wanted to get the topic off of him again. "So… do you remember anything about your life?"

"I do, but a lot of it is fuzzy. I remember bits and pieces, but I remember more now than I did when you first connected with me. Imagine my surprise! Going from a general feeling of timelessness, cold and dark to immediate light with vibrant colors and sounds. I remembered who I was immediately, and the memories of my life are slowly coming back to me."

"So, do you remember how you ended up there…in the ground?" he asked.

"No, I don't. That is a complete blank. It may come back to me; it may not. I am not sure. I know I didn't put myself there," she said, smiling.

"Why do you think you are still here? I mean…shouldn't you have 'passed over' or something?" he asked.

"What do you know about death?" she asked.

This caught him off guard because he didn't really know anything about the subject other than that people don't come back. "I don't know. I always thought there was a heaven or something."

"Well, I am in the same boat—I don't know either, but I do feel a tugging, like I'm supposed to be here for a reason or that I can't leave just yet. I don't know. It's hard to explain," she said.

"This whole thing is hard to explain," said Joe, talking aloud the thoughts that were running in his head.

"But hey—we are in this together! So, it's not all bad...right?" she said.

"No, I suppose not. I'm just glad I'm not crazy and something about all this does seem 'right' like it's supposed to happen," Joe said.

The gravity and uniqueness of the situation was blossoming in Joe's mind. He was perplexed by the forces that were in play here. What and why was he chosen to be a part of this experience? Was it happenstance; providence; or just plain, dumb luck-of-the-draw that he happened to touch those bones first? Or maybe he really was just crazy, and all of this was just an outlandish, vivid figment of his imagination. Deep down he knew it was not. For one thing, he had no idea what Mary looked like and the description that Mr. Brown gave fit the girl sitting in front of him to a "T." All these thoughts, and more, rammed through his mind within seconds.

"So, what are we supposed to do?" Joe asked.

Mary looked at him and said, "I think we are supposed to find out what happened to me."

"But Mary, no one knows what happened to you," Joe said.

"I know...I don't remember much. Like I said, it's all a bit fuzzy, but I do remember my last thought," Mary said.

"What was it?" Joe asked.

"I just remember being frightened and just scared...pleading out to anything or anyone that could hear my prayer—'Please, my mom needs to know'."

The memory of that last moment washed over Mary and tears welled up in her eyes, reliving the unknown fear and the sorrow. Joe, without thinking, moved to sit beside her and put his right arm around her and hugged her. He did the same thing for Andrew last summer when his dog died, and it seemed to help then. Mary turned her head into his shoulder and cried.

"Why did this happen to me?" she mumbled.

"I don't know," Joe said comfortingly, "but we will find out."

She lifted her head off his shoulder and looked him in his eyes with her own piercing, crystal blue eyes. "You really think so?"

Joe, not really sure, but wanting to comfort her said, "Sure I do...I mean...you said yourself that you are starting to remember more and between the two of us, I'm sure we can figure it out."

She leaned away from him and wiped the tears from her eyes, gaining control of herself again. "I'm sorry. I didn't mean to do that. It just came over me so quickly—that feeling of no hope."

"It's okay. I can only imagine, but you aren't alone now." Joe smiled, as he was getting more comfortable around her. "We are in this together."

She beamed at him, then gave him a smile of her own and said in a thankful voice, "Yes, we are."

Chapter Six

Minutes later, they found themselves walking away from Joe's house. They had decided that they should revisit Mary's old haunts (no pun intended), in hopes that it would refresh some memories. Before they left, he asked his mom to tell the boys, if they showed up to the house looking for him, that he was heading to the school yard where the town playground was located. It wasn't that far from his house, but he really wasn't planning on going there at all. He just didn't want to deal with the gang right now. He thought this would direct them somewhere else for awhile, so he and Mary could try to uncover some memories without distractions. His mom said that she would pass that along, but insisted he not to go too far if he did leave the playground and to stay close to home in case he started feeling bad.

But he was feeling better and better, so he didn't think it would be that big of a deal to travel within town. The first stop was the trestle in the woods where Mary's body was found. On the way to the location, they spoke of things they liked to do. Joe found out that Mary liked to read books…and none of that sappy stuff that a lot of girls like. She liked mysteries and thrillers! Joe thought this was great because he also loved to read those kinds of books and stories. She also liked to take photos and had been on the school newspaper staff, the "Pittsburg Howler." Unfortunately, due to the school enrollment dwindling, the journalism program was cut a few years back. Not enough interest or funds. Mary was sad to hear this news, because she had really enjoyed taking part in it. The more he listened to her talk about it, the more he wished he had the opportunity to do it, as well. The conversation was good; in fact, so good that time went by quickly and before they knew it, they were standing in front of the crime scene. The only things remaining at the site were footprints of the police and others in the mud and dirt, as well as remnants of crime scene tape tied to the tree. For the most part, any trace of any activity here was gone.

Joe looked at Mary and asked, "So, you remember anything here?"

"I'm almost scared to try. I'm afraid I might start crying again. Oh my gosh—I'm so embarrassed, but thank you for being cool about that," she replied.

"Well, we will never know if you don't try, so I'm here and it's going to be all right," he said.

"Oh, okay," Mary said.

She closed her eyes and looked to be thinking hard. After a few minutes, she opened her eyes and shook her head. "No, I am getting nothing. It's just blank."

"Where do you want to go next?" Joe asked.

"Let's head to my house," Mary said. "I would like to see my parents and I think there might be something there to help jog my memory."

"Okay," he replied.

Her house wasn't terribly far away. In fact, it could easily be reached through the woods they were standing in now. "Hey Mary, do you think you were heading home that day?"

"I can't remember right now. I mean…it's possible. Why?" she asked.

"I was just curious. If you travel that way," he said while pointing, "you get to the road and Mr. Brown's gas station. But that way, you can get to your house," Joe said.

"Mr. Brown! I haven't thought about him in such a long time! He was always such a nice man," Mary said, just remembering him when Joe mentioned his name.

"He is still the same," Joe said.

They walked in silence for bit. It was a nice day, considering. It was a bit hot but nothing out of the ordinary, and with a nice breeze flowing through the woods, it was pleasant. Mary just looked around and took it all in.

"You know, Joe, you never understand how beautiful this all is," Mary said.

"What do you mean?" he asked.

"This! All of this!" she said as she gestured to all around them. "The beauty of it all—the trees, the birds singing, the breeze—all of it. It's just all so important and something we take for granted. I never stopped once to take in the beauty of it all. And now that I have a second chance, I can just sit here and just enjoy the moment."

He listened to what she said and then looked around. He guessed he did kind of take it for granted. To be honest, he never thought about it before but putting himself in her shoes, he began to think about it from her perspective. She probably doesn't know how long this will last and so this really reinforces the moment for her. His heart went out for her. He had spent the majority of his time lately thinking about how weird this experience was for him but didn't take the time to think about how the experience was for her. He just watched her taking it all in. He couldn't help but to think how pretty she was and how much he enjoyed talking to her. It felt like they had known each other forever, even though they had just met. He had never experienced this before with any other girl. It just felt natural, he thought, which made him laugh to himself inside. "Yeah, it's natural all right—natural in a supernatural way."

They walked on until they turned off the trail and walked through the woods for a few dozen yards until they came to a field. On the other side of the field stood Mary's house, or rather, her family's house. It was light blue with a walkway going from the driveway to the steps and the front door. The front yard wasn't large and the front door was only a few steps from the driveway. There was one lone tree that would have been good for climbing, in front of the house. It had a wooden fence and a gate on the right side of the house.

They stopped and Joe heard Mary suck in her breath.

"Are you okay?" he asked.

"Yeah, it's just weird to me. You have to understand—it's like I was just here yesterday yet I also feel like it's been such a long time. The house and the yard have changed. The tree in the front yard was so much smaller..." She said, slowing down to take in all the other changes she noticed.

"I had a sister; do you know what happened to her?" Mary asked.

"I don't really know your sister but I know she still lives here, goes to the junior college over in

Avondale. Don't know what she is studying, though. Never really talked to her," Joe said.

"Oh, Joe—I just remembered! I used to keep a diary," Mary said excitedly.

"Yeah?" Joe asked.

"Yeah, but we will have to go inside to get it."

Chapter Seven

"What?" Joe asked.

"Yeah, it's hidden in my old room. Maybe it will give us an idea of what happened," Mary said.

"No—I mean, how are we going to do that? Just walk right on in?" Joe asked.

"Yeah," she replied.

"Listen, Mary, I don't want to be a spoilsport, but I don't know your family well enough to just stroll right on in, say hello and walk back to your room," he said.

"No silly—I know that. It looks like no one is home and I know where a key is…well, where it used to be," she said, then continued, "It won't take long, we will be in and out before you know it."

Joe didn't like this idea at all. What if he got caught? How would he explain all this? Thoughts like these were spinning around in his mind. But at the same time, he knew that if the answers were in that diary to help figure out what happened to Mary, then they had to follow through and get it.

"What if someone shows up?" Joe asked.

"We just won't get caught and the faster we move, the faster we can get out," she said. "Besides, my parents are pretty cool. I'm pretty sure they wouldn't press charges for breaking and entering."

"What?!"

"Just kidding! Come on. Let's hurry up."

Mary took a few steps before turning around to see Joe's hesitation. She then walked back and grabbed his hand to pull him along. "Come on!"

The house didn't have a car in the driveway and since it was the weekend, there's no telling where Mary's family was. They quickly crossed the field and stopped briefly at the street before crossing over. They looked both ways up and down the street to see if anyone was outside or nearby. Seeing nothing, they ran across and up to the front door. Mary pointed to a flowerpot on the front porch. Joe turned his eyes to where Mary indicated. The flowerpot was empty but there was potting soil inside, just enough to weigh it down. "There's a key underneath the pot, between the pot and the saucer," Mary said.

It wasn't very large, so Joe bent down and lifted the pot up. Sitting in the middle of the plate was a shiny, silver-toned key. Joe took one last look toward the street, as far as he could see in every direction, then bent down, picked up the key and unlocked the door. With one last sigh of resignation, he turned the knob, opened the door and quickly went into the room, which happened to be the living room.

"Mary, we haven't talked about this really, but do you think your room will still be the same?" Joe asked.

"I don't know," she replied.

The living room was separated from the kitchen by a bar with stools. There was a small dining room set in the area off the kitchen that could be seen from the front door. It wasn't a very large house and it wasn't all that different from Joe's house. In fact, all the houses in Pittsburg weren't that big except for a few…and even those weren't huge. There was a hallway immediately to the left leaving the living room. Mary took the lead and headed down the hallway. Joe still couldn't believe he was doing this but he followed her.

They passed a couple doors on each side of the hallway. The first door on the left was open and by briefly looking at the decor, Joe assumed it must be Mary's sister's room. Mary continued to walk to the end of the hallway, coming to a stop at the last door on the left. She indicated that this door led to her bedroom.

"I'm scared, Joe," Mary said.

"Why?" he asked.

"I've been gone a long time and if my room isn't the same as I left it, I feel torn between being sad and being happy. Because the thing is—if my room is different, then that means they've moved on, which makes me sad because maybe they forgot about me. But if my room is the same, I'm also sad because they haven't moved on and still worry about me. I would have never wanted my family to go through something like this," she said.

"Well, we'll never know until we open this door," Joe said.

He immediately opened the door, almost like quickly pulling a Band-Aid off a scrape. He figured it was better to do it fast and get over the pain quickly than it was to go slowly, with the pain persisting. The room looked like it did twelve years ago. Mary's mom had left it untouched since her disappearance, with the hopes that one day Mary would return. The bed was made with a yellow comforter set and everything else in the room was clean and neat. There was a chest of drawers on one side of the room and a desk on the far side of the wall, underneath the window that looked into the front yard. There was also a sliding closet door leading on the wall that was shared with the room next door. Mary's mom must have dusted the room weekly because there was no dust build-up on any of the surfaces to include the nooks and crannies of the furniture.

Mary sighed. "I don't know whether to be happy or sad. I'm so full of mixed feelings."

"Mary, it's okay," Joe said. He really didn't know what to say but felt that he needed to say something. He could have made a better effort to speak, but it was time to get back to the task at hand. He didn't want to be there any longer than he had to.

"So, where is your diary?" he asked.

"Oh, it's right over here. I kept it hidden. I didn't want my little sister snooping on me," she said. She went over to the dresser and pointed almost behind it, down to an air vent that was near the floor. "Right here."

Joe went over and got down on his knees for a better look. Just a normal vent with sliding latches that kept it in place. Not a bad hiding spot you could get to quickly. He undid the latches and looked inside.

"It's not here," Joe said.

"What?!" Mary said.

"Just kidding—it's right here," he said as reached in and pulled out a dusty Ziploc that had deteriorated over time. There was a small book inside, too large to put in his pocket so he just held it in his hands. He put the vent back in place and stood up.

"All right, let's get out of he..." Joe was about to finish before he heard car doors slam outside, then voices that sounded as if they were coming from the small walkway approaching the front door.

"Oh crap, they're home!" Joe said. "What do we do?!"

The door to Mary's room was still open when they heard the front door opening and could hear her parents talking.

"Did you forget to lock the front door?" Mrs. Teller asked, talking to her husband.

"No. I don't think so, but maybe..." he replied.

Joe quickly crossed the room and shut the door to the hallway, leaving the rest of the conversation muffled. They could hear her parents coming and going. When Joe looked through the window, he saw that they were bringing in groceries. Joe could feel the fear creep up inside him as the blood to his face pumped wildly. He didn't want to get caught. How on earth would he explain why he was there? Somehow the thought of trying to explain that he was talking to the ghost of a dead girl, and "Oh, by the way, it's your dead daughter that made me break in" would sound worse than just saying he was trying to steal something…even with the backlash he knew he would get from his own parents.

Mary indicated toward the closet sliding door. "Get in there," she said.

"What? Why?" he asked.

"Because, if you want to get out of here, I have an idea. Get into that closet," she said.

Joe slid open the closet door slowly so it wouldn't make a sound and revealed a very organized closet with clothes hanging neatly, a few small boxes on the overhead shelf and shoes along the bottom. Though there was room, it didn't go very deep. The wall stopped immediately behind the clothes. Joe looked at Mary questionably, there was nowhere to go, looking in from the door. They would be found immediately, he thought.

Mary just crouched slightly and gingerly moved the clothes aside as she went in and moved left of the door and out of sight. Before doing so, she looked at Joe and mouthed the words, "Come on," before disappearing. Joe followed, trying his best not to trip on the shoes and other stuff on the floor. Mary told him to close the door behind them, which he reluctantly did. "Great," Joe thought to himself. Now they were going to be in the dark…in the closet of a room he wasn't supposed to be in, in a house that he didn't technically "break" into, but somehow explaining the use of the key to open the door didn't seem like it would help. Once he closed the door quietly behind him, the closet became dark and it took a moment for his eyes to adjust. Slowly, he realized there was another light source further down the closet and he realized that he was in a very small hallway. The two rooms, Mary's and her sister Samantha's, were connected by this single closet. There was a door from the closet to each room and split by a few feet of this closet hallway, but no walls separating them. He immediately thought of secret passageways from the mystery books he enjoyed reading.

"This is why I had to hide my diary. I couldn't lock my door and my sister could just sneak in, anytime she wanted. But it was kinda cool because when we were younger and closer, we would play way past bedtime without our parents knowing." She smiled. "Those were good times."

This had all transpired in a few moments. Mary's parents were still in the process of bringing in groceries from the car. Mary and Joe could still hear them as they talked, apparently the subject of the unlocked front door forgotten. Mary stopped at the opening to the next room.

"Okay. I am going to go out there in the living room. We have to hurry though, because they are probably almost done. We have to time this right…once I'm out there and when they're both outside again, I am going to shout "Go!" When I do that, run into the kitchen. There is a side door that you can leave from. Got it?" Mary asked.

Joe, not wanting to make a sound, only nodded that he understood. Mary turned and left the closet and headed out of the room. A few seconds passed by but to Joe, it felt like hours. He looked at the bag with the diary in his hand. This better be worth it, he thought.

"GO!"

He felt like a scared rabbit that was just startled and his heart started pumping wildly, even more deeply in his chest. He had to be quick but not quick enough to stomp—surely Mary's parents would hear that, so he moved at a reasonable pace so as to not make sound. He left the closet and quickly went through Mary's sister's room into the hallway. He heard Mary's parents outside. "Is that the last of it?" Mrs. Teller asked.

"Yup," Mr. Teller replied.

He heard the trunk door slam outside. Joe didn't stop. He had to get through the living room before they made it to the door. With that thought in mind, he picked up the pace and since it wasn't a large house, he ended up in the kitchen a half second later. When he rounded the corner into the kitchen, he saw Mary beside the door that led into the fenced-in backyard. He ran up and turned the knob. He could hear Mary's parents almost to the front door. He opened the door quickly and slipped out. He closed the side door just in time as he heard the front door close. His heart was still beating rapidly in his chest and he was gulping for air. His legs suddenly felt like rubber, but he managed to stay upright. He wasn't out of the woods yet...or rather, *into* the woods. He thought that would have been funny at any other time. They still had to hop the fence without being seen. He crouched and moved under the kitchen window, hugging the wall so he wouldn't be noticed, even by accident, as he moved toward the front of the house.

"Wait," he heard Mary say to him.

He stopped and looked at her, still not wanting to say anything for fear of getting caught.

"I...I just want to pop in real quick to look at them. Just give me a few seconds. I haven't seen them in a very long time and would like to see how they are," she said.

Joe immediately thought that was an absurd request, as he didn't want to get caught, but before he said anything, he pondered it some more and completely understood what she was asking. He thought, if roles were reversed, how could he not take a few moments to see his parents after all the time away? He just looked back at her and nodded his head.

"Thank you!" she said, smiling and then quickly disappeared back into the house. She went straight through the door like it wasn't there. "So strange," he thought, "but then again, what about today hasn't been strange?" He got back to paying attention to not getting caught. Although it was only a few seconds (which seemed to take three times as long to Joe), Mary reappeared. She wasn't smiling and had a pensive, almost perplexed, look on her face.

"Okay, we can go now," she said.

"Are you all right?" he whispered.

"Yeah," she said somberly." It just wasn't what I expected, but we can talk about that later. We need to get out of here first."

She then broke out into a smile and led the way toward the front of the house, over the fence and safely back into the woods across the street.

Chapter Eight

Under the shadows and safety of the trees, Joe suddenly felt extremely tired and while breathing heavily, collapsed next to a tree along the trail. His heart wasn't pounding as much as it had been and now that the danger of being caught was gone, he was coming down from his adrenaline kick. He looked up at Mary. "I don't want to do anything like that ever again."

"Oh, come on—you didn't get caught. That was fun!" she exclaimed.

"No. No it wasn't," Joe said. All pretenses of bravery were now gone. Normally, around other girls, he would have felt the need to act like a "man" but in the company of Mary, he felt something that he had never experienced with anyone else, even his guy friends. He felt he could be totally honest and open with her. "That scared me."

"I know. I could see it all over you face!" She laughed, but then she stopped laughing and more empathetically said, "You did great. You were very brave."

That made Joe feel good.

"And we now have my diary. Hand it to me," she said.

He looked down at the Ziploc bag with her diary inside. He was still clutching it and honestly, with all the commotion of leaving the house, he had forgotten all about it. As he looked at it, he became confused.

"What?" he asked.

"Hand me my diary," she said. "I don't want you reading it. I have no idea what's in there. I can't remember and I don't want you to read something embarrassing, okay?"

She held out her hand expectantly. Joe handed it to her and she took it.

Still confused, Joe asked a stream of questions, trying to wrap his head around what he was experiencing. "Wait a minute. How can you go through solid doors but still grab that diary? Did you even need me to go into that house? Couldn't you have done that on your own? And what if someone saw you now—would they see a floating book? How are you doing that?"

"It's magic," she said, but then added, "I don't know. I didn't make the rules. I just know what I can and can't do. And no, I couldn't go into that house alone without you. For some reason, I have to stay close to you. I can't just go anywhere and when it comes to you, I am pretty sure I can only touch you and things you have touched."

"That's so weird," Joe said absentmindedly.

"Well, duh. Of course it is. Imagine being me experiencing it—it's even weirder," she said.

She sat down beside Joe and it was true, he could feel her next to him. She was just as real to him as anyone else. Mary took the diary out of the bag, opened it up and started skimming through the pages. Joe, recovering from his momentary exhaustion, looked over and saw the neat handwriting on the pages but couldn't read it from where he was sitting.

It was late afternoon/early evening now but during the summer, the days went on forever, and they still had plenty of daylight left. He watched Mary as she intently read a page or two, then flip a couple pages to read more on another page. In the back of his mind, he had the inkling of a thought that would grow over time; he wished that she wasn't a ghost and that she was alive. She suddenly laughed.

"What is it?" Joe asked.

"Oh nothing—just something funny I wrote. Now I remember something that happened to my sister and me," she said.

She looked over at Joe and could tell he was still curious. "Ok fine, I will tell you, but it's probably not going to make sense to you."

"Samantha and I, when we were younger, went to a family reunion and there was a variety show that all the family members—aunts, uncles, cousins—could participate in. So, Samantha and I thought we would have a comedy show. We practiced our jokes and then when it came time, we got up in front of everyone to do our show. Only, it wasn't funny. I mean, the jokes were so bad and our delivery was absolutely horrible. No one laughed...but then, everyone started laughing, but not because our jokes were funny, only because it was so bad that it was comical. So, I guess in the end, it worked out. We still made everyone laugh...just not how we thought we were going to. We never did another show after that," Mary said.

"Oh, I wish I could have seen it," Joe said.

"No, you don't. I wouldn't want to subject you to such torture," she said while smiling. She continued, lost in thought, "But still, it was a good memory."

"You know, it's so strange...those are my parents back there," she said, indicating toward the area and the house they had just left. "But they looked so different."

"What do you mean?" Joe asked.

"Just that, I have this memory of what they looked like and while they look familiar, they look totally different. I guess it would be similar to seeing your parents one way, going to bed, then waking up the next day and they suddenly look very different. Of course, I recognized them but they had more wrinkles and just looked kinda sad. I don't remember my parents with that look before. It was just so…unlike them," she said, then looked at Joe again. "And thanks for taking a moment to let me see them."

"Of course," Joe said. "I'm not gonna lie. At first I was just wanting to get out of there, but then I thought if it were my parents, I'd like to see them."

"You know," she said, still looking at Joe but now she looked at him like she was discovering a new bug. "You are different from all the boys I remember. You are thoughtful, and I like that."

This gave Joe a different kind of energy. It perked him up and he smiled at her, which she returned. Suddenly feeling awkward, he asked, "So, find anything out?" nodding toward the diary.

"I just started, silly, and no I haven't…at least not yet," she said, "but the more I'm reading the more I'm remembering, so that's good."

It wasn't long before they could hear the gang of Joe's friends riding their bikes, whooping and yelling on a road nearby. Joe got very still. A part of him wanted to go join his friends immediately, but there was a tiny part of him hoping that they wouldn't find him. As quickly as the sounds came, they were fading in the distance as the boys passed on by, going on some adventure elsewhere. Judging by the direction that the noise was heading, Joe believed they were heading to the Catholic church with the graveyard, on the outskirts of town. They would usually play there. They never did anything harmful to the cemetery and they even took care to not step on the grass over any of the graves…that was super disrespectful. They just enjoyed hanging out there because there always seemed to be a nice breeze that flowed through the cemetery and church grounds, even on a hot steamy day. Also, for boys with active imaginations, it was a great place to have adventures.

"Sounds like your friends are having fun. Don't you want to go join them? Mary asked.

"No…it's okay. I'd rather stay here and hang out with you," he said.

To Joe, Mary seemed to like that answer. "Good, because we gotta find out what happened; I don't know how long I have here."

"What do you mean?" Joe asked.

"I don't know. I just feel that time is very limited," she said.

Deep down, Joe didn't want to hear that. He knew what was going on was special…well, weird, but also special. And for the first time ever, he actually felt completely comfortable around a girl without feeling dumb. In the back of his mind, he vaguely knew that whatever this was, it obviously couldn't last forever, but he hadn't really thought of the possibility until she brought it up.

"Oh," he said, then after a few moments, "Well, we better make the most of it and find out what happened to you."

The time went by rather quickly for Joe and Mary on that little trail in the woods. They had continued to talk about life, memories, and anything else that would pop up in conversation, including the rabbit trails that they would go down together. Joe told Mary about the time he was boating down the river at a church camp and accidently fell out of the boat. He was rescued shortly thereafter but he thought he was a goner. Joe felt like he had never talked to anyone like this before, including his best friend. Strangely enough, the same thought was going through Mary's mind, as well. She remembered her friends vaguely as though through a fog, which indeed, as she read more of her diary, that fog wasn't as thick. But even in those memories, as close as she was to those friends, this experience and her friendship with Joe felt different.

Joe looked up and saw that the sky was darkening. It was way past dinner time—funny, he didn't even notice. He looked at Mary and said, "We gotta be getting back. My parents are going to get worried."

"Let's go," she said.

They both walked slowly down the path that would lead them out of the woods and eventually back to Joe's house. Halfway home, Joe felt the need to say something about the events of the day, from meeting Mary to all the other events, even the ones that scared the bejesus out of him. "For what it's worth, I really enjoyed today," he said.

"I did too."

Chapter Nine

They arrived at the house and went inside. Joe's mom told him that the food was in the refrigerator and needed to be heated up if he wanted any. He went over to the fridge and saw that it was chicken and green beans, a staple for the Anderson family. He quickly prepared and warmed up his meal. He didn't want to take long, as he wanted to hurry to the safety and privacy of his room so he could talk with Mary some more. He felt rather rude because Mary was standing there watching him this whole time, remaining quiet since she knew he couldn't talk openly to her. Shortly thereafter, Mary sat on one of the stools and turned her focus to her diary saying, "Take your time. Go ahead and eat. I'll just continue reading over here."

His mom came into the kitchen, saw him and asked a couple of questions, from how he felt to how his day was and then followed those with asking if his friends ever caught up to him. He quickly looked to see if his mom noticed a diary just floating there in Mary's hands, seemingly without any support, because she couldn't see Mary. It looked as if she didn't even notice it. "Strange," he thought to himself. Turning his attention back to the question at hand, without going much into it, he replied that no, he didn't get up with his friends and that his day was normal for the most part. He didn't want to lie to his mom. He didn't like lying, period, so instead of saying anything untrue, he just avoided anything that would lead to a lie.

"Oh yeah? What wasn't normal about it?" his mom asked.

"Oh shoot," he thought to himself.

"Oh, nothing crazy." That was a downright lie and he inwardly scolded himself, then quickly added, "I was just lost in thought most of the day."

He thought, "well, a little truth can't hurt" and continued, "I walked around and really just kind of thought about that girl that we found in the woods."

He saw Mary look up at him from her diary with a mischievous grin, a grin of knowing exactly what he was doing. He was being truthful without being truthful by talking around the subject. She winked at him and went back to reading.

"Yeah, I can imagine," his mom said. "It's the talk of the town right now."

She then trailed off and looked at Joe. "I can only imagine what you feel right now since you found her."

"Oh yeah, I found her all right," he thought to himself.

"Mom, I just don't understand how anyone could do such a thing to such a pretty girl," Joe said. "Oh no! Now I went too far!" he thought. He didn't even realize what he had said until it came out of his mouth. "Oh…I mean, I heard she was pretty."

His face started flushing because Mary was right there and heard him. His mom didn't notice his face reddening as she was washing the dishes and looking outside. Joe could feel it in his face and was relieved his mom hadn't noticed. But then he looked at Mary and she was staring at him.

"You think I'm pretty?" Mary said, knowing that Joe couldn't answer, so she just broke into a smile.

Joe felt like a scared rabbit, and probably looked like one too, he thought to himself.

Thankfully, Joe was saved when his mom replied, totally oblivious to the exchange between Mary and Joe. "I don't know son. The world doesn't make sense sometimes and it can be a painful lesson to learn…but let's not think about that right now."

"Mom, what is everyone saying?" Joe asked.

"Well, it's not official yet though everyone is pretty sure that it is the Tellers' daughter," his mom said.

Joe knew this because he was looking at the Tellers' daughter right now. His mom continued, "Speaking of which, we will have to make some food and take over to the Teller family sometime this week. I'm sure they are going through so much right now. Your father told me that the sheriff stopped by this afternoon to talk to them. They hadn't heard yet, which is surprising, since everyone in town was talking about it. I guess no one was brave enough to talk to them about it. My heart breaks for them."

Joe quickly finished his dinner and washed the plate. Even though it was early evening, he told his mom that he was tired and going to go to his room to read before going to bed. As soon as he entered, he shut the door, then immediately leaned up against it and let out a sigh.

"So, you think I'm pretty, huh?" Mary asked.

"Uh...well, yeah," he replied, trying to act nonchalant but failing miserably at it.

"Well, I think you are kinda cute too, well for a young'un," Mary said, almost laughing.

"Wait a minute—I'm not that much younger than you," Joe said defiantly. He was about to continue, but then he remembered at the same time that while Mary was only a little older in her current state, had she been alive still, she would be in her twenties. The look on his face reflected Mary's as the same thought crossed her mind. The thought of that silenced them both and the moment quickly became awkward with Mary finally breaking the silence. "Well, I've pretty much read all through my diary and I'm not any closer to figuring out anything about what happened to me. I remember a lot more, though, and hopefully the memory of that day will come back. But at the same time, I am also scared of remembering it."

"So, nothing?" Joe asked, glad the conversation took a turn off the awkwardness and back onto a subject they could talk about.

"I really enjoyed photography. I liked to hang out at Mr. Brown's convenience store. In fact, I think I was there the day I disappeared. I'd go there all the time because I enjoyed watching people come and go."

"Hey, I like to do that too!" Joe said.

"Aren't we an exciting town..." she said sarcastically, with a grin, "where generations of kids enjoy seeing people come and go?"

Joe laughed at this, then added, "Well, it sure beats living in Bolt!"

"Oh, I know!" she agreed.

Bolt was a smaller town, not even a village, a few miles away. If anyone thought Pittsburg was slow, Bolt was even slower. And there were always healthy rivalries between the small-town kids to the point that even those Bolt kids would say "Well, it beats living in Pittsburg."

"What does your last entry say?" Joe asked.

"It says that I planned to make a day of taking photos around town the next day and was going to stop by Mr. Brown's store to grab something to drink. I knew I'd get thirsty, so I made a note so I'd remember to take some money with me. I had also planned to meet with someone at the school that morning. I don't know why I didn't write down the name. I guess I thought I would remember." She grimaced, which even on her face, was still cute. "Sorry, it doesn't really help," she finished.

"Sure, it does," Joe said. "Where did you like to go take pictures?"

"All over. Maybe the meeting had something to do with the school newsletter."

"Well, the town isn't big. We'll figure it out," Joe said. "We could stop by and talk to Mr. Brown again, to see if he remembered you saying anything."

"That's as good as anything else right now," she said.

"Well, we have to go to church in the morning, so maybe tomorrow afternoon, we can go see him," Joe said.

"Sounds good to me," she said.

They continued to talk until it was bedtime, which came faster than the both of them realized. As Joe got ready for bed, he didn't undress like he normally would have because he wasn't used to having an audience, he thought.

"Do you sleep?" he asked.

"I don't know. Today is the first day and I'm not sure. Maybe I sleep when you sleep," she said.

"Well what happened last night?" Joe asked.

"I sort of phased in and out; I think maybe I am tied to your consciousness. Maybe that's why I'm tired now—because you are tired. Last night, I would phase in when you were close to waking and kind of fade when you weren't," Mary said.

"That makes sense," Joe said. It totally didn't, but it seemed plausible enough.

"Do you want to sleep on the bed?" he asked. "I can take a blanket and sleep on the floor here."

"And how would you explain that to your parents if they happened to come in?" Mary asked, smiling at the thought.

"I would tell them the truth. I have an imaginary friend who is in my bed." He smiled back.

Mary laughed. "I bet you would."

"Well how about this, we will take turns each night. I'll take the floor tonight and you can have the bed; then, tomorrow night we will switch. I'll just set the alarm to wake up before my parents come in to wake me, so they won't be curious seeing me on the floor," Joe said.

"That works," she replied and hopped on the bed.

"This is a comfortable bed...you sure?"

"Yeah," he replied.

"It's been ages since I have felt this comfortable lying down. Thank you Joe," Mary said.

The sincerity in her voice made Joe's heart and soul sing a little. "Oh, no problem. I am glad you feel good," he said.

He quickly left the room to go tell his parents "good night" and that he loved them, then came back, again closing the door behind him. "I used to do that as well. Every night I'd tell my parents 'good night' and that I loved them. In fact, every time I was on the phone or leaving the house, before I said goodbye, I would always make sure to say 'I love you.' Of course, I learned it from them. You just never know when it's the last time you will see someone," she said.

Joe didn't know how to respond to that, so he just said, "Yeah, it's important to tell people how you feel about them."

Joe took a blanket and lay on the floor. The carpet was thin and a little rough and the floor was hard. He had two pillows, one he gave to Mary and one he kept for himself. He took the lamp from his table, along with his alarm clock, and put it beside his head, then set the alarm for 7 AM. Church didn't start until 11 and Sunday school went from 9:30 to 10:30. His parents would usually wake him up at 7:30 Sunday mornings but like he told Mary, he didn't want his parents finding him on the floor and asking questions he didn't know how to answer. He was about to turn off the light but before he did, he said, "good night" to Mary, who didn't respond. He got to his knees to look at her. She was fast asleep. He took a moment to look at her sleeping. He knew that he had just met her but down deep, he felt like he had known her forever, a feeling he never felt before. It didn't hurt that he thought she was pretty, and she looked like an angel sleeping. He took another quick moment to savor the view, lost in thought, before lying back down and turning off the light. Before long, he was asleep as well.

Chapter Ten

The alarm clock rang, and Joe slapped at it instinctively. For a second, he didn't know who or where he was; he just felt stiff and a little uncomfortable from sleeping on the floor. He quickly remembered everything that transpired the previous day and he jumped up to see if Mary was still there. She was, and was waking up too, yawning. She looked at Joe through eyes that were gaining energy and said, "That was great. I haven't rested like that in a long time."

"That's good to hear," Joe replied, then asked, "So, uh...I need to use the bathroom and take a shower. You uh...staying here?"

He suddenly felt foolish at the thought, but he didn't want to undress and do his business in the bathroom in front of her. It made him uncomfortable. She grinned mischievously back at him. "Maybe..." she said.

"Uh..." he began.

"I'm just kidding. I won't look." She winked and then added, confidingly, "Everyone needs privacy at times, and I'd be the same way."

"Oh good," Joe said, suddenly feeling relieved as the pressure, that he hadn't realized was there, lifted off his shoulders. From his chest of drawers, he grabbed clothes he planned to wear to church, then left the room only to run into his mom in the hallway on the way to take a shower.

"What?! You're up early on a Sunday. Who are you and what have you done with my son?" she said.

Joe laughed it off. "No, I just felt like getting up early—that's all."

"That and I didn't want to complicate things worse than they already are," he thought to himself.

"Well, good. Breakfast is almost ready," she said as she left him, heading back toward the kitchen.

He quickly went through the morning routine of getting ready for the day. Today would probably go down in the books as finishing in record time, because in the back of his mind, he didn't want Mary to get bored and maybe come surprise him. He would die of embarrassment, he thought. He quickly dressed and returned to his room.

"Feel better?" Mary asked. "You sure took that shower quick. You looked like you were in a hurry. I can't believe I saw you like that!"

86

Joe's blood froze. "But you said you weren't…" he sputtered.

"I'm kidding! I didn't. I stayed right here," she said as she smiled and laughed at Joe's obvious discomfort.

"That's not funny!" Joe said.

"Oh, come on! You have to admit it was…a little," Mary replied.

Joe wanted to be mad, but couldn't, as he did love a good joke. "Yeah, you got me—it was a little funny," he conceded.

A short while later, Joe was at the kitchen table eating breakfast, which consisted of scrambled eggs and toast. He also had a large glass of cold orange juice which tasted great as he guzzled it down. The family then piled into his mom's car, a small blue sedan, and headed to church. Mary sat beside him in the back seat. He could feel her next to him and he wanted to talk to her but obviously couldn't with his parents less than a foot away in the front seat. Mary sensed what he was thinking and just winked at him with a grin.

They attended First Baptist Church of Pittsburg, again, the only Baptist church in town, which was only a couple blocks away from the house. He knew he would see his friend Matt in Sunday school. Johnny and his brother Frankie attended the Methodist church in town so they wouldn't be there, and Andrew didn't go to church, which Joe thought was strange. He had gone to church so long that he didn't think there was an option of not going. It was just something you did. Not that he would have wanted to not go, because he actually enjoyed it. It was nice to see everyone. Everyone was friendly and every so often the church would have potlucks with fantastic, home-cooked food. He loved Mrs. Winter's deviled eggs when she was alive. Mr. Winters didn't come to church much with her when she was alive and didn't come at all after she had passed away. He wondered if Mary's parents would come to church today. With everything going on in regard to Mary's body being found just a couple days ago, he suspected he wouldn't see them, but adults are weird, so who knew?

After they parked, he said goodbye to his parents and headed toward the back of the church to where the Sunday school classrooms were located. Matt rushed over when he saw Joe. "Hey man, what happened to you yesterday?"

"What do you mean?"

"Your mom told us where to find you and you weren't there."

"Oh, I was just in the woods." And that was true but, in his mind, he thought about the fact he was also breaking and entering Mary's house, but didn't feel like bringing that up.

"Well, you missed out. We headed over to the Catholic church and had a great time. We also heard more stories about that girl's body we found," Matt said.

"Oh yeah?" Joe asked, perking up.

"Yeah. Everyone went home to eat and since it's the talk of the town, everyone's parents were talking about it. So, we all talked about it when we got back together," Matt said.

"What are they saying?"

"Well, there are a couple of ideas that people seem to think happened. A lot of people think that Mr. Brown had something to do with it. Of course, our parents didn't include us in the conversation…most of this we just happened to overhear while they were talking to one another. They said that he had a weird "vibe" around girls. I don't know what vibe means but whatever, I've never seen Mr. Brown do anything weird."

"Yeah," Joe agreed.

"The other idea was something to do with the school, since she was always there…and then the last thing that people are talking about was that it was a crime of opportunity committed by someone who lives here or someone that was traveling through."

The thought chilled Joe. The thought that the murderer could still be living in town was just unthinkable to him. Like oil and water not being able to mix, his thoughts felt the same; he just couldn't comprehend such a thing. He looked at Mary, who was listening in, as well. She didn't indicate toward any of those ideas being true, but she couldn't remember, so any one of them could be. She just looked at Joe and shrugged her shoulders. She didn't know any more than anyone else...at least, not yet.

Sunday school came and went. Joe was lost in thought for most of it and wasn't paying attention. When he got to the church sanctuary, he noticed that Mary's parents hadn't come. There was no one sitting in the place they usually sat. During the church service, he liked to sit up front with Matt and the other church kids but today, although he sat right before the preacher, he wouldn't remember any of what he said or even the topic of the sermon. He couldn't keep his mind from running all over the place, thinking of possibilities. The unknown is a large territory to cover when you don't know what you are looking for. Mary sat beside him and he had a strange thought: Mary used to come here and sit in the same pews, listen to the same sermons, have the same conversations with her friends. The only thing that separated them was time...and the great divide of life and death. Heavy stuff for the mind of an almost fourteen-year-old, he finally concluded. The church service ended with the usual alter call, where the preacher invited those that wanted to learn more about the Lord as their personal savior and those who just wanted to come up to the front and pray. Every head was supposed to be bowed and eyes closed, but he noticed Mary leave his side and go to the front to kneel at the altar and pray. When it was over, she returned to his side and he noticed her eyes were red from crying. He wanted to comfort her immediately but knew that if he did, it would look strange to those around him, putting an arm out and hugging empty air. Since he couldn't do that, he did the next best thing—he stepped closer to her and put his hand on top of hers on the top of the pew, then leaned in and whispered, "Are you okay?" She looked up at him through her bloodshot, no longer teary eyes. Now she was recovering. She nodded her head and gave him a weak, but grateful smile. At any other time, she probably would have been embarrassed, but their relationship had grown greatly over the past couple of days and she felt okay to be real with him. He smiled back at her warmly and squeezed her hand. He had surprised himself that he would be so bold to even grab her hand like that in the first place, but immediately knew it was the right thing to do, especially with the feedback he had received. He liked making her feel good; it made him feel good as well. The feeling, as well as the moment quickly passed, and reality set back in. The preacher brought the service to an end. After closing, everyone filed out of the church and into the parking lot.

It wasn't a big church and the congregation wasn't large so it never took long to leave. There were always some who would stay back to visit each other and catch up or gossip about what was going on in town. Today seemed a little more active in that respect, which seemed to be in response to the news of the girl's body being found. Joe could feel some of the adults slide their eyes his way, looking at him as he walked by. He couldn't tell if it was different than any other Sunday, because people glanced at each other all the time. However, since Mary was there and he had the whole situation on his mind, he was more self-conscious this morning than usual. He quickly left the sanctuary and went outside, Mary following.

Matt came up and asked if Joe wanted to hang out that afternoon with the guys. Joe declined, saying that he had some stuff to do but didn't go into it. Matt kind of looked at him weird. They always hung out on the weekends and this was definitely different from the norm.

"Are you sure? You feeling okay?" Matt asked.

"Yeah, why not?" Mary heard the whole conversation and jumped in, talking to Joe.

"Yeah, Matt. I'm fine. I just have to get some other stuff done," Joe said while looking at Mary pointedly.

"Like what? Maybe I can help," Matt said.

"Sure! Why not ask him to come help?" Mary continued talking to Joe.

"No!" Joe said sharply to Mary, but it came out a little too sharply toward Matt. When Joe realized it, he added, "I'm sorry Matt. I didn't mean to be short. I just have some things I gotta do around the house." Then said to himself, "That, and I have to figure out who murdered Mary and I can't do that with you tagging along." He then looked at Mary as if to ask, "Why did you do that—just join the conversation knowing I couldn't respond?"

Matt's dad called out to him to come back inside and help with the after-church cleaning, which saved Joe from the awkwardness of the conversation. With that, Matt looked back at Joe and said, "Fine. You've been acting weird lately, you know."

While running back inside, Matt stopped at the door, turned, and looked questioningly at Joe before disappearing inside. Joe walked over to the family car and waited for his parents to show up so they could go home. Joe thought to himself, "Oh boy, Matt, you don't even know the half of it."

Now that Mary and he had a moment alone while waiting for his parents, he let out a breath. "Wow, it's been so hard not to talk to you this morning and…what was that all about? You knew I couldn't answer you openly."

"Oh really? It wasn't hard for me at all," she said with a wicked grin, but giving Joe a look that let him know that she was joking. She added, "I know, but I wanted to see you in the hot seat a little."

Joe was quiet for a moment then Mary spoke up and said disarmingly, "I'm sorry, I only did it because I like you."

"I like you too, but please don't put me in that position again. It's hard enough without letting people know that I might be crazy," Joe said.

"You aren't crazy," Mary said.

After a moment, Joe replied with a smile, "Maybe I am…but I like it."

Joe thought about the end of church service and had a burning desire to ask. "Mary, you don't have to answer but back there during church, what did you pray about?"

Mary's smile quickly left her face as she looked off in the distance. "I don't know why I did that. It just felt right. Then I got up there and I just got so mad and asked God 'Why did all this happen to me and my family?' He didn't answer… but I did feel a peace about everything after I let my emotions get away from me. I don't know. It's hard to explain."

It wasn't long before Joe's parents showed up. "Ready to go, kiddo?" his dad asked.

Joe was more than ready to get back home. "Yep!"

They piled back into the car and headed back to the house. Joe ran inside quickly but slowly enough to tell Mary to wait outside his room while he changed out of his church clothes and put on something more suitable to run around outside in. Not that church clothes and play clothes were too much different in a small town like Pittsburg; it was more along the lines of the best of the regular. Some men and boys would wear button-up shirts but for the most part, it was a nice shirt and the best jeans you had. Since families weren't made of money, they'd change back into their "work" or "play" clothes since they knew they were going to possibly get dirty. Those "good" clothes were for the civilized. At any rate, Joe wasn't thinking much on this; it was more or less a habit for him. It didn't take him very long and he linked back up with Mary, who was waiting patiently.

As Joe and Mary rushed out of the house, his mom asked, "Do you want lunch?"

"No thanks. I'm not really hungry. I think I'm going to go the school playground and hang out," he said.

"Didn't you do that yesterday?" she asked.

Without answering the question, he just said, "Well, it's a fun place to hang out and pass the time. What else am I going to do?"

"Are you meeting anyone?" she asked.

"I don't know. I haven't made any plans...but the town is only so big and I'm sure the rest of the guys will show up at some point." He secretly hoped they wouldn't so he and Mary could continue their investigation without interruption.

"Well, just be careful—and you come home straight away if you start to feel funny like you did Friday," she said.

"Will do, mom," he replied and with that, he was out the door with Mary trailing.

When they were at the edge of the yard, Mary said, "I like your mom. She seems so nice."

"Yeah, she is great. So is my dad," he said.

"I'm sure. They both kind of remind me of my parents," she said, then frowned and sighed. "I guess I'll never talk to them again..."

"Hey! Don't think like that!" Joe quickly said. "I tell you what, maybe we can write a note to them after this is all over...or...or..." but Joe couldn't think of anything else to say that would help or even be possible.

"I'm okay," Mary said. "I was just letting my thoughts get the better of me. Let's get going."

It was true that the playground by the school was a destination they had in mind but first, they were going to stop by Mr. Brown's store and ask some questions. When they arrived, the store looked empty from the outside. No cars were parked in the spaces or at the pump and no customers were entering or leaving. They walked inside, with the bell behind the door ringing as they did. Mr. Brown was not in his usual spot behind the counter. The little radio behind the counter was playing some 50s rock and roll station. Just like it looked from the outside, the inside was indeed empty…which felt strange to Joe. He could have just grabbed anything and run, but he wasn't the type of kid to do such things (though the thought did cross his mind). He looked at Mary and Mary back at him, and they both just shrugged.

Joe walked over to the counter and noticed the door to the back of the store was slightly ajar, from his position, he couldn't see beyond. He called out for Mr. Brown, but no answer came. Concerned, he walked closer to the door and called again.

"Maybe he's not here," Mary said.

"No. He's always here," Joe said.

"Well, he isn't here now," she said.

"He's gotta be," he replied.

Joe slowly opened the door to the back. He'd never been back here but it opened to a small office area. The desk was cluttered with all kinds of record books and receipts. He looked around and saw that the office had a hallway that went off into darkness. He could make out boxes of inventory stacked up against the wall. He could barely see another door at the end of the hallway. He slowly walked closer and was about to open that door when he heard a toilet flush on the other side, then the door abruptly opened. Mr. Brown appeared, staring down at Joe.

"What the heck son, can't you leave a man in peace to do his business?" Mr. Brown said. "What are you doing back here?"

"I...I..." Joe sputtered, totally shocked and embarrassed.

Mary started laughing out loud.

"Well, spit it out son," Mr. Brown said.

Joe didn't know there was a bathroom back here; he only knew of the one on the other side of the store. He just looked back at Mr. Brown, finally calming down enough to say, "I called your name and no one answered. I...I got worried and decided to check on you."

"Yeah, I heard you but thought I'd be done before you came walking back here. As you can tell, I was sorta busy. With people coming and going, I gotta answer nature's call sometime," Mr. Brown said.

They walked back out into the store area and Mr. Brown looked around. "Where's your friends? I couldn't make out what you were saying but I thought I heard you talking to someone."

Joe realized that Mr. Brown heard him and Mary talking, and quickly answered, "Oh, I was just talking to myself out loud."

"So, you're here by yourself?" Mr. Brown asked.

"Uh…my friends should be here shortly, at least they said they would be," Joe lied. He immediately felt bad about not telling the truth, but then all those stories Matt had told him that morning about Mr. Brown came to mind. Only then did Joe realize that no one knew he was there. That was dumb. Just then, the bell on the front door rang as a customer came into the store and greatly relieved Joe. Good; at least someone saw him here, but he still had to ask Mr. Brown some questions. The customer only came in to get some cigarettes and a lotto ticket then left just as quickly as they had come, leaving Joe alone with Mr. Brown again.

"Well, what can I do for you?" Mr. Brown asked.

"I wanted to ask you about Mary Teller," Joe said.

"What?" Mr. Brown said. "We just had a conversation about her yesterday. What's got you so concerned?"

"I don't know. I just can't help myself; I can't get her off my mind," Joe said, which was true, especially when she was standing there looking as real as anyone else he knew.

"Well, like I said yesterday, she came here quite a bit, but that's not surprising, because all the town kids come here," Mr. Brown said.

"She was here the day she disappeared, right?" Joe asked.

Mr. Brown narrowed his eyes through his glasses at Joe. "How do you know that?"

"Just something I heard. You know how this town is. Everyone likes to talk about everything," Joe said.

"That's true enough," Mr. Brown replied.

"So, do you remember that day?" Joe asked.

Mr. Brown took off his glasses and cleaned them with the bottom of his shirt. As he was cleaning them, he looked up and his face got a faraway look, as he was delving deep into his memory.

"Yeah, I do vaguely," he said. "And she did come in here the day she disappeared. She liked to hang out here and I liked her…a lot."

Joe remembered the stories of Mr. Brown being a little weird toward young girls, which at first, he thought was silly but listening to him now, he wasn't so sure, so he dared to ask, "Why?"

Coming back to the present, Mr. Brown asked, "What?"

"Why did you like her…a lot?" Joe repeated.

Mr. Brown put his glasses back on and put his hand to his chin as he looked distant again. He then looked at Joe as if making a decision. "Well, I'm going to let you in on a little secret. Although, I'm sure half the town knows already. I didn't always live here."

"Really?" Joe asked, not sure where this conversation was headed.

"Yup, I lived upstate—closer to the big cities. I also had a family, a wife and a daughter at that time." As he spoke, his voice got a little more somber. He continued, "They were my everything. This was…oh…back in the 50s. But there was a fire in the apartment building where we lived. They didn't get out and burned to death. I was working as a traveling salesman at the time and was away."

"Oh…I'm so sorry," Joe said.

"Oh, that's horrible," Mary said beside him, listening in.

Mr. Brown looked at Joe. "It's okay, son. It happened a long time ago but Mary Teller, and to be honest, a few of the other girls that have come in over the years, have reminded me of my little girl, Donna. She was bright and beautiful just like that Teller girl. About the same age when it happened, too."

The weight of the room became heavy with somber memories of better times and better people. Even Joe, being as young as he was, could feel it. Then Mr. Brown moved on and the weightiness of the conversation lifted. "But anyway, that's why I remember that she came in that day."

"The day she disappeared, did she say anything?" Joe asked.

"No, not really. It was a quick visit. She came in that day mid-morning to grab a soda. Said she had been out taking pictures with that camera of hers and was parched…then she was heading on to take more photos."

"Hmm…" Joe said, mulling it over in his mind.

"Then she left, and that was it. I heard the next day that she had disappeared. Talked to the sheriff and everything. It's weird, son—whenever something like that happens to a girl like Mary Teller or to my little Donna, or anyone you care about, afterwards, you always wonder 'what if?' What if I had talked to her more? What if I made sure she got home safely? What if I had stayed home for my little girl and my wife instead of traveling? Sometimes, I think these kinds of 'what if' questions one has about different situations have a haunting of their own…and in some cases are worse than an actual haunting, I'd suspect."

Joe looked at Mary and although it was weird, he kind of liked the haunting, though he had never really thought of this as a haunting until Mr. Brown said the word. Joe knew Mary wasn't alive but it sure was hard to grasp that she was dead, when she was right there having conversations with him. In the back of his mind, he knew it couldn't last, but he wasn't in a hurry for the end to come because he really enjoyed her company. He then looked back at Mr. Brown and said, "Thank you for being so open with me, Mr. Brown."

"Well, with the look in your eye, you look like you needed the truth. I don't know what you are up to, but I hope you find whatever it is you are looking for," he said.

A few minutes later found Joe and Mary walking away from the store. "So that's why he was always so nice to me. I had no idea," Mary said.

"I didn't either. He could have been lying, though," Joe said.

"True. We will have to look and see if his story checks out," Mary said.

Mr. Brown watched Joe through the front window of his store as he walked away. He wondered about what the kid knew or if he stumbled across something regarding Mary Teller. That kid seemed to have an air about him that was different than usual. As he watched Joe disappear back into the heart of Pittsburg, he thought he saw Joe talking to himself. Nah, must have been his eyes playing tricks on him, he thought to himself. He then walked to the back of the store; may as well take advantage of the slow afternoon to stock shelves. A few minutes later, Mr. Brown thought no more about Joe…or anything else for that matter. Mr. Brown was dead.

Chapter Eleven

Fifteen minutes after leaving Mr. Brown's store, Joe and Mary were at the playground, which was right beside the school they both attended...well, the one Joe attended and Mary had attended when she was still living. It was a small school and getting smaller by the year. It looked ancient though, constructed of brick and stone. The playground beside it reflected its appearance, with the same type of building material. The benches, the small amphitheater and some of the other fixtures had the same brown stone with white plaster holding it all together. Very sturdy and picturesque. It even had a circular walkway with a small—very small—fountain in the center, which probably could have held goldfish if one were inclined to place them.

"I always liked this area," Joe said, making conversation.

"Same. I liked to get on those swings over there and jump. I felt like I was flying, even if it was only for a little bit," Mary said.

"Ha! I did too until I hurt my ankle once," he said.

The playground and school grounds were kept up by the school janitor and groundskeeper, Mr. Daniels. He had worked there longer than Joe could remember. Mr. Daniels kept to himself. He was the town…well, not "drunk," but not because he didn't drink. He did but Joe thought that calling him the town drunk was a bit too harsh; he was definitely a ne'er do well. Mr. Daniels' saving grace, if he had any, was that he did do a good job of keeping the grounds in repair and looking somewhat decent. Joe never really talked to him, nor had any of the other kids. He kept his distance and so did they. Joe only thought about this because he noticed him walking by the school and to the house next to the schoolyard, where he lived.

Mary was looking at the school when Joe turned his attention to her.

"Anything?" he asked, hopefully.

"Nope," she replied, "other than the normal memories I have of this place. Wait—something vague is coming up."

"Oh yeah?" Joe said.

"Yeah, I wanna say that I met with Mrs. Johnson that day; she was the advisor for the school newsletter and I'm pretty sure that was what the meeting was about. I think Coach Dill was there too, but it's not a clear memory. It's like seeing something through a fog; it's there but you can't really make it out."

"Mrs. Johnson is going to be a problem, "Joe frowned, "she moved away years ago."

"That's too bad. I was hoping to see her. She was a great teacher," Mary said.

"But tomorrow is Monday. We can stop by and talk to Coach Dill. It's still early enough in the summer where they are cleaning out their classrooms and preparing for the next year," Joe said.

"Really?" Mary asked.

"Well, yeah, I mean, as long as I can remember, the teachers here always stuck around for a bit longer. Now, if we had wanted to talk to him in a couple weeks, he may not be here. He likes to take his family on a vacation later on during the summer break," Joe said.

"Sounds good, we will come back then," she said.

They spent the next twenty minutes talking about school and some of their memories of it, which was a struggle for Mary, but she enjoyed listening to Joe talk about his memories. He told her how once he had been in a school play, but the whole class hadn't taken the time to memorize their lines. It wasn't long before everyone on stage looked like scared rabbits.

The teacher, Mrs. Beckett started reading lines from off-stage in a loud whisper where everyone could hear. He then explained that while this was going on, he was on stage and couldn't hold in his laughter because in his mind, he couldn't believe how stereotypical of a school play this had become. It worked itself out and all the kids got through it, but Joe never volunteered again for another play, which was fine with him.

"I wish I could have been there. I bet that was funny," Mary said.

"Yeah, it w…" Joe was about to reply but they heard sirens coming in from the distance and it sounded like it was coming from the direction of Mr. Brown's store. They looked at each other and then back to where they came from.

"Let's go see what that's about," Joe said and started to head that way. Mary didn't miss a beat and followed. A few minutes later found them back in front of Mr. Brown's store. Being a small town, any commotion brought attention, so a small crowd of folks that had the same idea as Joe and Mary, had gathered to see what was going on.

The sheriff's cruiser had since turned off the siren and was parked right in front of the gas station's door with the lights still flashing. It had bold lettering down the side of the car with the sheriff's badge in the middle of the door. There was another small, blue car at the pump which was the only thing that looked normal…or at least felt normal. It wasn't long before a second deputy showed up, then a third. Whatever was going on, everyone in the county seemed to want to be involved, as two more cruisers showed up shortly thereafter, with an ambulance not far behind. The last deputy walked into the store and then back out to tell people to stay back, as he set up a taped perimeter.

The townsfolks of Pittsburg sure thought it was getting strange there, seeing that two events that caused half the county law enforcement to show up, happened on the same weekend. The first event, of course, was the one with the Teller girl and now this, whatever happened at Mr. Brown's gas station. At least that was the general consensus and conversation of the small crowd that gathered at the perimeter, watching the scene.

"Someone said they heard a gunshot," said a guy in a red shirt and blue jeans, talking to another lady or anyone who would listen.

Joe didn't know that man very well but he knew everyone that had gathered, at least by sight, even if he didn't know their names.

"Was it a robbery?" another person asked aloud.

Mary looked around and then at Joe. "I'm going in to see what happened."

Joe only nodded and thought that was a good idea since no one would see her. When Mary entered the store, she got a really bad feeling. The deputies were moving all around. Two deputies had a lady to one side of the store, interviewing her about what she had seen.

"I came in to pay for my gas, and the gas attendant wasn't around. I saw that the door to the office was wide open and there he was, on the ground. That's when I used the store telephone to call you guys," the lady said.

"Are you from around here?" one of the deputies asked her.

"Oh no. I live in Avondale and I was on my way to Jamestown City, but then I saw that I needed gas and this one is the only station for a few miles," she replied.

Mary walked past them to the office where she immediately regretted what she saw. She saw Mr. Brown's body lying there in a pool of blood. There was a gunshot wound to his head and there was a revolver by his hand on the floor.

Sheriff Mattson arrived and walked into the office.

"What do we have here, deputy?"

"Well, sir, it looks like it might have been a suicide," the deputy replied.

"Hmm…that's strange. Known this guy for years. Any notes?" the sheriff asked.

"No sir."

"Well, do a thorough walkthrough, and dust that gun for prints. Also, send one of the other deputies outside to interview the people gathered and ask if anyone saw anything."

"Yes sir," said the deputy, then left, leaving Sheriff Mattson alone.

"Very strange," he muttered before heading back out of the room to go help the other deputies.

Mary watched him walk out of the office and the deputy that left returned to retrieve the revolver. She looked down at the body of Mr. Brown, then looked back up and noticed Mr. Brown standing there, looking down at his own body. He looked up at her, almost surprised. "Mary Teller, what are you doing here?" then looked back down at his own body again before continuing, "I guess I really am dead."

"Mr. Brown, I have to know. Did you kill yourself?" Mary asked.

"What? Heavens no! Why would I do such a thing?" he said.

"Do you remember what happened?" she asked.

"I was going to do inventory. I then heard or felt a presence of someone in the room with me and when I turned to see who it was. Then I felt this immense pressure in my head. And now, here I am talking to you. I didn't see who did it," Mr. Brown said, frowning.

He looked at her again and said, "I'm surprised to see you here. I thought it would have been someone else here waiting for me."

"I haven't crossed over yet, so I don't know," Mary said. "I'm still figuring out what happened to me, which is why I think I'm still here."

"Oh, I'm so sorry. A lot of us wondered what happened to you. So, you don't know what happens next?" Mr. Brown asked.

Mary shook her head no.

"Well, I don't really care about what happened to me. I was old. I was just waiting to die anyway but I don't want people to think I killed myself. I would have never done such a thing."

"I'll make sure that gets known," Mary said.

He looked at her earnestly and asked, "You will?"

"Yeah, for some reason, Joe Anderson can see me. In fact, I was here with him when you saw him this afternoon. He is helping me and we will make sure that people know the truth," Mary said.

A calmness flooded Mr. Brown's whole demeanor. "Oh, that's great! I'm so relieved. Thank you so much."

Mary looked at him and noticed he had a strange look on his face as he looked past her, at something she couldn't see. It was a look of wonder as his eyes got bigger, seeing whatever it was that she wasn't seeing.

"Oh Mary, it's so beautiful," he said.

Tears of joy came to Mr. Brown's eyes as he reached his arms out to the unseen. "Oh! Donna is here…and so is my wife. I've waited so long," he said.

Mary just watched as he enveloped his arms around something that Mary still couldn't see, almost as if he was hugging someone. Then, with a look of a pure elation on his face, the outline of his figure glowed a soft, white light that intensified over a couple seconds, until his whole being glowed, then ebbed until he faded into nothing. Mary could still detect the shape of the glow for a little while until that, too, faded away.

Joe was still outside, observing the whole thing. He saw his dad's friend, the sheriff, talking to the other deputies. The crowds had grown quite a bit for a small town; news travels fast. A local news crew showed up in a van marked "Channel 3 News" and set up near the crowd with a cameraman and a reporter. This was the first time Joe had seen a news crew show up anywhere, so he walked closer to get a better look. It wasn't long before Sheriff Mattson went over to the reporter and agreed to answer questions.

"Sheriff Mattson, can you tell us what is going on here today?" the reporter asked. She was wearing a blue skirt suit and looked every part the professional reporter, which seemed a little out of place in the small village of Pittsburg.

"Well, this is an ongoing investigation and we are still determining what happened."

"Was this a robbery, or a murder or…" the reporter interjected.

"At this time, we do have one deceased male. Although, it looks to be a suicide, we haven't ruled out anything at this point."

This last little bit of information led to a collective gasp throughout the crowd that was close enough to listen. Mr. Brown had been a local fixture for years, and even though Sheriff Mattson didn't say his name, everyone knew it had to be him.

The reporter continued, "Sheriff, with the body rumored to be that of Mary Teller being found a couple days ago, do you think there is any connection."

The sheriff replied, "I am not aware of any connection but if there is any, I am most certain that we will find out through our investigation."

The reporter continued to pepper the sheriff with more questions, each of which he replied professionally to. Joe heard some of crowd near him speculate that with Mr. Brown being found dead by possible suicide, maybe he had something to do with the Teller girl's disappearance. It seemed to make the most sense, with her body being found on Friday, that he killed himself on Sunday because he thought the investigation may lead to him. It was an interesting theory that Joe was beginning to wonder about before Mary showed back up.

"Mr. Brown's story checks out," she said.

"What?" Joe asked, then realized he was in the middle of the crowd and thought it might look weird if he was talking to air. He grabbed Mary by the hand and lead her away to a more secluded spot and asked again, "What do you mean?"

"Well, Mr. Brown is dead," she said.

Hearing a confirmation of this news shocked him. It was one thing to hear the sheriff mention finding a body inside, because it could have always been someone else, but finding out it is a person who you knew most of your life is something else entirely.

"Seriously? What happened?" he asked.

She explained what she saw inside, the conversation she had with Mr. Brown and what she had observed when he left, which all left Joe a little speechless. He just received a huge dose of information that, mixed with the shock of everything else going on, left his mind feeling sluggish in trying to process it all. Well, at the very least, he could inform the sheriff. He told Mary that he was going to go to tell him that Mr. Brown didn't commit suicide. He paused as he was on the way to get the sheriff's attention because he didn't know how to approach the subject without making it sound weird. He steeled himself and decided to go forward with the idea anyway. Better to just get it out there. He went back to the perimeter where the station had been taped off and waited until he saw the sheriff look out toward the crowd, which was now starting to dwindle. No matter how interesting something was, it was still a summer day and one could only stand the heat for so long. Joe waved at the sheriff to get his attention and thankfully, Joe thought, he noticed. Sheriff Mattson walked over and asked, "What are you doing Joe? You ok?"

"Yes sir," Joe said. His parents had always taught him to be respectful with good manners and say his "sirs" and "ma'ams" no matter who he was talking to.

"Well, Joe, I am kind of busy, what do you want?" the sheriff asked. He liked Joe, being his friend's son, and he was a nice kid, he thought.

"Sir, I just wanted to tell you that Mr. Brown didn't kill himself," Joe said.

The sheriff tilted his head and looked closer at Joe, "What makes you say that?"

"Because we were...I mean, I...was just here before it happened. I think I might have been the last person here before...well...you know, this happened. And he said he was on his way to do inventory," Joe said. Which wasn't a lie because he did tell Mary that's what he was doing. Joe then continued, "And I don't think anyone who plans to go do inventory is going to kill himself."

"That does make sense, Joe, but we'll see what the investigation reveals," the sheriff said, thinking it over but then thinking about Joe. "You've been through a lot this weekend. You sure you're okay?"

"Yes sir," he said again, assuring the sheriff that he was fine.

"All right. Well, I am going to have one of my deputies come over here and ask you a few questions."

"That will be fine," Joe replied.

The sheriff turned and started to walk away, but then Joe suddenly remembered something else. "Oh Sheriff—one more thing," Joe started. The sheriff stopped and turned back, "When Mary Teller disappeared, did you ever find her camera?"

The sudden shift of topics and the question itself both surprised Sheriff Mattson. He walked back over, kneeled down and put out a hand on Joe's shoulder for support, but to also get a better look at Joe's face. "Well, no. We never did. We assumed we would have found it where her body was, but it wasn't there either. How did you know about that?"

"I've been asking a lot of questions and Mr. Brown told me that the day she disappeared, she had her camera with her, so I was just curious," Joe said.

"Huh," the sheriff muttered to himself as he thought it over, then responded to Joe, "That makes sense. That's good detective work son. But...uh...don't go around asking too many questions. A lot of weird stuff going on. If whoever is responsible for that little girl's disappearance is also responsible for Mr. Brown's death...I don't know at this point if it is or it isn't, but in the off-chance that it is, I don't want anyone else to become a target, okay?"

"Yes Sir," Joe said.

Sheriff Mattson looked once more into Joe's eyes to make sure his point was taken, then squeezed Joe's shoulder as he got back to his feet.

"Good. Now wait here a little bit while I go get a deputy over here to ask you those questions."

It wasn't long before the deputy came over and asked Joe about his visit with Mr. Brown that morning. It was general questions like what time he arrived, what time he left, what did they talk about, etc. Joe answered as best as he could. Mary just stood there beside him, waiting to help him out if he had forgotten anything, but there really wasn't much to forget about an interaction that occurred a couple of hours ago. As soon as the deputy finished asking his questions, he flipped closed his notebook and thanked Joe for his time.

Joe looked back at the crowd and noticed all of his friends were there. In the back of his mind, he was surprised it had taken them that long to show up. They saw him talking to the deputy and kept their distance, but as soon as the deputy walked away, they swarmed him and stepped on each other with questions.

"What was he talking to you for?" Johnny asked.

His brother Frankie asked, "What happened here?"

Matt said, "What did you do?"

And little Andrew asked, "Are you okay?"

Of course, all these questions were coming at him all at once, with more questions to follow, in an enthusiastic fashion you'd expect from a group of young, almost teen, boys. When the excitement came down a notch, Joe tried to answer the questions he remembered.

"Wow...Mr. Brown...dead," Andrew said with a little shock. "I can't believe it."

That was the common response in Pittsburg over the next few days, for all those that knew Mr. Brown. He wasn't a celebrity by any stretch of the imagination but now that he was gone, it would be strange, kind of like having a picture on a wall for years, then all of a sudden it's gone. It becomes strangely noticeable.

Joe let them know that he had been there shortly before his death but didn't see what had happened. The other boys concluded it must have been a suicide, because who would do such a thing? Joe still voiced that it was murder but didn't push it too much, as he didn't want to get into the argument of how he knew. It would just lead to other questions that he didn't feel comfortable talking about right now with them, if ever. While they were talking, Joe saw Coach Dill show up in the dwindling crowd, but he didn't stay for very long before he, too, left. Joe wanted to go talk to him right then, but couldn't figure out a way to get away from the group. If he had, the others would have just followed, and he wouldn't have been able to ask the questions he wanted to. Mary just kind of hung out near him, not saying anything, but every once in a while, they'd share a knowing glance and either smile or roll their eyes, knowing they couldn't talk until they were able to get away by themselves again.

"What are you doing?" Johnny asked.

"What—me? Nothing," Joe replied, knowing he had been caught making a face when he thought no one was looking.

"You keep looking in that direction and making googly eyes," Johnny said, indicating the direction where Mary was but since he couldn't see her, he pointed through her.

"No, I'm not," Joe said.

Johnny just looked at him suspiciously. The other boys were engaged in conversation of another topic and hadn't noticed what Johnny and Joe were talking about. "Joe, you are not a very good liar. You never have been," he said.

Joe felt his cheeks flush. "I know. I just can't talk about it right now. I just have a lot on my mind right now."

"Well, you don't have to go through it alone, Joe. We are all here for you," Johnny said.

"Thanks, man. I really appreciate it and one day I will tell you guys everything but right now, I can't talk about it until I can figure it out myself," Joe said.

This seemed to satisfy Johnny, at least for now, and he turned back to the other boys and started talking with them. Joe felt bad because he wanted to include his friends, but sincerely felt that this was something that he would never be able to tell anyone. How could anyone understand it? Or they would think differently of him if he had tried to explain it and they didn't understand. How can you tell your friends that you are developing feelings for a...ghost?

"You got caught," Mary chided and then gave him one of her beaming smiles. Knowing that he couldn't respond just made her smile bigger.

Chapter Twelve

Later that evening, Mary and Joe were back at his house. It was dinner time and Joe was at the table, eating dinner with his parents. Mary took this time to go to Joe's room to peruse her diary some more, in hopes of reviving some more of her memories. Midway through dinner, the conversation had died down a little, but Joe hadn't participated too much in it, as he was thinking of other things, like Mr. Brown, Mary, and what had happened to her camera. Joe's parents noticed that he was keeping quiet, then his dad broke the silence. "I talked to the sheriff. He called about an hour ago to see how you were doing. He told me that you were at the store shortly before Mr. Brown was found. Is that true?"

"Yes, sir," Joe said.

"Want to talk about it?"

Joe's attention quickly focused on the current conversation. His mom looked surprised. "You didn't tell me that you were heading there. I thought you were going to the school and playground."

"Well, I was, but I wanted to stop by there first," Joe said, but he didn't really want to get into the reason why. "It's sort of on the way."

Which was sort of true—if you went out of your way. He could tell right away that his mom wasn't buying that and appeared to be gearing up for further questions that, surprisingly, never came. She just reiterated that even though Pittsburg was a small town, they needed to know where he was, because the world is a dangerous place. In this fact, he agreed. Joe looked back to his father who was still looking at him, waiting for an answer to his question.

"Uh...no, not really. What's there to talk about?" Joe said.

"The sheriff told me that you thought what happened to Mr. Brown wasn't a suicide and that you were asking some other questions. All I am saying is, you've gone through a lot this weekend. It's okay to talk about it, about how you feel. You keep that stuff bottled up and it can mess you up."

Joe knew he couldn't or wouldn't talk about everything, but he did want to get a little bit off of his chest. Once he started though, it was like a runaway train, since he was bursting with emotion. He didn't talk about Mary though, but he did talk about how he felt about what happened to her and what his thoughts were regarding Mr. Brown. He questioned how anyone could do such a thing to Mary and to Mr. Brown, if it wasn't suicide. The more he thought about it, the more it hurt him but it also made him angry. Tears came to his eyes, not in a sobbing way, but in a quiet intensity. He was experiencing feelings of helplessness in a situation over which he had no control, because it was something that happened in the past. This made it all the more sorrowful because he knew how sweet and amazing Mary was… or to him, at least. All of her possibilities…her future was taken away. It was gone and that weighed on him more than he knew. Of course, he kept that last part to himself.

He pushed away from the table when he was finished and said he was going to go to his room. His parents watched him walk away and were saddened themselves that they couldn't do anything to help in this situation, except to offer support and care. At some point in everyone's life, sometimes more than once, they come to a place that changes them and they knew that Joe was going through one right now. Life and reality come in different forms that can smack one across the face and if one is not careful, can dim the light in anyone's eyes. They hoped that this wouldn't be the case with Joe.

Joe closed the door to his room behind him and Mary was seated in the corner of the room, still reading her diary. "How was dinner?" she asked absentmindedly, still paying attention to her diary.

"It was okay."

She looked up and smiled at him with her full attention.

"I wish I could eat; I'd love to have a pizza!"

Joe quickly bottled up the sorrow he felt from the conversation he had earlier and smiled back at Mary. "Me too! I can always eat a slice of pizza."

"We have a lot in common, you and I," she said.

"I like that," he said.

"Me too," she agreed.

They settled down and talked for a little while, covering different topics that were only important to the minds of young teenagers. But whatever they talked about, there was genuine laughter. Later that evening before bedtime, Joe noticed lightning outside, through his window. He grabbed Mary's hand and dragged her outside to watch the show. Way off in the distance, the clouds were building, and lightning continued to flash between the different clouds at a steady tempo. They both sat down on the steps in front of the house and continued to watch. Across the field, the lightning bugs started to emerge. Now, Joe had always called them lightning bugs but he also heard other people call them fireflies. He liked seeing them because they would light up the night like snowflakes drifting through the air. And with the lightning bugs beneath the storm clouds in the distance, it made the scene very picturesque. The temperature dropped and it was almost perfect. In fact, at that moment, with the view and with Mary by his side, Joe didn't want it to end. Mary seemed to be enjoying the experience, as well. But all good things must come to an end and before long, it grew dark and was time to go to bed.

When they returned to Joe's room after he told his parents goodnight, he turned toward Mary. "You get the floor tonight," Joe said, as he playfully smiled at her, as if he had an upper hand in an argument they weren't having.

"I know," she replied with a smile that reflected his own.

As they lay down, and just before sleep, Mary thoughtfully asked, "Do you think we will find out who did this to me?"

"Well, yeah. We have to. Do you think I want you haunting me forever?" As soon as he said it, he realized he didn't mean it the way it sounded.

"Oh," she said.

"I'm sorry. I was trying to be funny but it wasn't," Joe said.

"It's okay," she said.

"But I think so. Eventually your memory will come back and we will know."

"Yeah, I know," she agreed. "I was just thinking out loud."

It wasn't long before they were both asleep but an hour later, the storm that had been building off in the distance arrived and a loud clap of thunder startled them both awake. Mary's memory was still hazy about the day she had disappeared but one thing she did remember is that it happened during a storm. This caused her anxiety levels to rise.

"Joe?" she asked.

"Yeah?"

"Um…can I sleep up there with you?"

There was a pause in reply that eventually came, "Uh…" Joe began.

Mary interrupted to explain, "It's just that…I'm embarrassed to even say this, but storms scare me."

"Sure," Joe replied and moved over to make room for her.

She moved to the bed and lay beside him. Joe could feel her presence next to him and although he was nervous, he liked it. He didn't like storms that close either, but it was nice to have her next to him. Another flash of light brightened the room, followed by a loud clap of thunder that jarred them both. Since they were both wide awake, Joe asked her if she was all right. She was, but then wanted to share a memory with him.

"When I was a little girl, I had a dog named Max. Max and I would go stay with my grandmother during the summers and when bad storms came in, my grandmother would let us sleep with her. So, I guess this kind of reminds me of that—safety."

"Where's your grandmother and Max now?" Joe asked.

"Oh…they are both dead," she said, then continued, "My grandmother died of old age when I was nine and Max…well, he was run over by a car."

"Oh, I am so sorry," Joe said.

"Yeah, that happened when I was eleven and it was one of the worst days of my life. I loved that dog. In fact, after losing him, our family didn't want to replace him because the pain was so bad. So we never got another dog after that."

Joe could only imagine. His mom was allergic to animals, so he never had a dog or cat like other kids his age. But as he was listening to Mary talk about her dog, he didn't know if the fact that he didn't have a dog was a good or bad thing. That's a lot like life though, he thought to himself—one never really knows what decisions are good or bad until after the fact. His dad would always talk about hindsight being 20/20 and that experience is where wisdom comes from. He wondered, though, is the wisdom always worth the experience? Deep thoughts, which fortunately or unfortunately, were put to the side when another lighting strike hit close outside. This one was closer than any of the others and the thunder clap that followed was immediate, causing them both to jump and instinctively grab on to one another. They were almost blind due to the flash, and about deaf due to the closeness of the strike. When the excitement of that moment subsided, they realized they were still holding onto one another. This caused them to momentarily stiffen but neither one was letting go, so they both slowly relaxed. They could feel the closeness and the heat from one another and that brought comfort in unexpected ways for them both. Eventually, Joe felt like he had to say something—anything—but that moment came and went and the longer he didn't say anything, the harder it was to think of something to say. He started to overthink and then felt really awkward, but was saved when he realized that even with the storm raging outside, Mary had fallen asleep. He could hear her deep but relaxed breathing. Lightning flashed a few more times in the distance and lit up the room. Joe looked to confirm she was sleeping and took the moment to just look at her, as he had done the night before. She was so beautiful and in the back of his mind, he wished beyond reason that things were different—that she could have been born later or he earlier, and that they could be "real" friends or possibly even more. He knew that wasn't the case and it never would be. The reality, even though harsh, was that no matter how close they got, there was an end coming. But even as he knew this as truth in the back of his mind, he also thought in, childlike wonder, "Well, I don't know that for sure, so we can just enjoy it while we can." He watched her sleeping for a little while longer before sleep overtook him too.

Chapter Thirteen

The storm came and went and by Monday morning, the sun was beaming with blue skies all around, though the weatherman said there may be another line coming through that afternoon or evening. The sun blazed through the window in Joe's room, waking him up. He found that he and Mary were still holding each other. Joe usually slept peacefully but something about last night made it even more peaceful. To avoid awkwardness before she woke up, he attempted to withdraw his arms, causing Mary to wake up. And since he was in the process, his arms were still around her. She opened her eyes and looked directly at him, then her eyes widened, too, as she realized the same thing that Joe had. Well, so much for avoiding awkwardness.

"Have we been like this the whole night?" she asked.

"Uh...yeah, I believe so," Joe said.

"Oh," she said quietly and thoughtfully as if she were processing the whole situation.

Joe began, more to fill the silence than anything else, but also to justify their sleeping position, "I'm sorry…I didn't mean to…The lightning and everything and before I knew it, we were asleep."

Mary interrupted, "Oh no, that's okay."

She let out a little laugh, "I mean, I was there too. And it felt safe."

This tidbit of information gave Joe butterflies, but more along the lines of excitement that he couldn't quite put into words. He had felt the same way—safe. Again, he didn't really want it to end but the sun was up, and he knew they had to get up.

"Well, I better go take a shower and get ready, so we can head over to the school to catch Coach Dill," Joe said.

"I guess so," Mary said.

Joe got up and grabbed Mary's hand to help pull her up. "But Mom! I don't wanna go to school," she said playfully.

"Ha! I have said that more than a few times, and yet every time, I end up going," he said.
"Well stay here and I will be right back," he said, while gathering what he was going to wear today, as he left to go about his daily, morning ritual. Of course, in line with yesterday morning, he didn't take long. He still didn't want Mary to come waltzing

in to surprise him. He didn't think she would, but girls are weird, and he didn't know how much he could trust her, especially if she got bored. This was also one of the things he found charming about her. He liked the way they bantered back and forth. There was enough stability and variety in the conversations that they had to stay interesting, even exciting at times. He enjoyed learning more about her and her memories as they came to her. He also enjoyed sharing his thoughts with her. Over the past couple of days, he had shared things with her that he had shared with no one else. He couldn't get over how easily they bonded and how quickly the time had passed since meeting. But he didn't dwell on it terribly long because again, he didn't want to be caught with his pants down...to which he laughed quietly to himself. He hurried through the rest of the routine and was dressed and ready to go in just a few minutes.

When he got back to his room, he found Mary staring out the window into the yard. He looked beyond her and saw nothing out of the ordinary, just some birds flitting around some bushes in the yard.

"You just never realize how much you take for granted. I know we talked about this the other day but it's just so true and I'm reminded of it all the time now," Mary said.

Joe was caught off guard by the seriousness, or maybe regretfulness of the tone. Not understanding what she was talking about, he asked what she meant.

"You always hear, "Stop and smell the roses." From what I remember, I never took the time to stop and smell the roses. Just like those birds outside, I never stopped to just watch them," she said.

"Well, you were a kid...I mean..." Joe started, not knowing where he was going with this, but continued to try and come up with an explanation. "I'm sure when we get older, we do stop to enjoy the roses."

"I'm not so sure, Joe. I think it's one of those things you have to be aware of and the only reason I am now is because..." she stopped abruptly, with her eyes suddenly tearing up.

She turned away from Joe to hide her face, but Joe saw the tears before she could. The only thing he could think to do was give her a hug. And even though he was a little fearful to do so, he mustered some bravery so he could bring her some comfort, or at least show that he cared. So, he came up behind her, wrapped his arms around her and gave her a hug. With his face over her shoulder, he could smell the sweet scent of lavender that he noticed the first few encounters they had together. He could also feel her; she was so real to him.

"Well, think of it this way—now you know," he said. "I don't know this for sure, but I bet some people never get this lesson, ever."

And sensing that she was really concerned about the future she had lost, Joe continued, "And who knows—maybe this lesson will help you going forward wherever you go next, whatever that experience is."

As he said this, he also couldn't help getting the feeling of, or a sense, of loss. Before he could dwell and before his own eyes started to water, Mary turned toward him and returned the hug. He could feel her whole body squeezing into him, which took his breath away in more ways than one.

"Thanks," she said.

She let go and the hug between them was over.

"It didn't help, but at least you tried," she said, smiling at him. She was back to herself again.

"And besides, if we stay here dwelling too much on the past or future, we missed the whole lesson of being here in the moment, right? Come on. Let's get going," she continued, and with that, she left the room on a mission. Before they left the house, Joe took a moment to tell his mom where he was going and explain that he wanted to go up to the school to ask Coach Dill something about the sports program for the upcoming school year.

"Really?" his mom asked. "You've never seemed interested before."

"Well, I am not overly interested but I wanted to go hang out at the playground. I know my friends will show up eventually and since I will be there, I figured I'd ask Coach Dill about it if I see him. Just wanted to let you know where I was going."

"Oh…uh…okay. Well, you know the drill. Be careful and don't go anywhere without coming and telling me first," his mom said.

"Okay Mom. Love you," he said, as he grabbed a couple pieces of toast heading out the door. Mary was waiting for him outside and they headed toward the school and playground.

"What do you remember about that day? Anything new?" Joe asked Mary while they were slowly walking. They were in no hurry; they were more or less strolling, just enjoying each other's company.

"Not much more. It was during the school year, and I had to meet Mrs. Johnson that Saturday morning for the school newsletter. I had an assignment that she wanted to follow up with me on. We were going to talk about it Friday afternoon, but she got tied up with classwork that she had to take care of. She asked that if I wasn't busy on Saturday morning, could I come by the school, so I agreed. I arrived early that day and waited. I vaguely remember Coach Dill being there but it's still not totally clear."

"What was the assignment?" Joe asked.

"Oh, it was just some fluff piece on some school club. I took some pictures and wrote a story that she wanted to go over in depth."

It was still rather early in the day. The sun had only been up a couple of hours when Joe and Mary walked into the school yard. Coach Dill hadn't arrived, as his car wasn't in the parking lot but again, it was still early. Joe told Mary that they could wait and see. He usually shows up around this time, from what he knew and heard. She replied that was fine and they could just hang out until he did, which suited Joe just fine. In fact, it wouldn't have bothered him if Coach Dill never showed up. There'd be plenty of time to go talk to him eventually. Right now, he was just really enjoying the time he had with Mary.

Clouds were starting to build up in the distance to the west. Joe saw it building rather quickly and he knew that there would be a storm before too long, by the looks of it. So much for being out and about all day. They'd have to return home soon, but they still had some time to wait before it reached them.

While they waited, they sat on the swings and swung back and forth. Joe looked up and noticed the groundskeeper, Mr. Daniels, watching them from his yard. It was hard to see him clearly. He was standing just to the side of the bushes, near the entrance to his house. He was just watching them—or him, rather.

Joe was about to comment on it but he then heard a car coming down the road. He turned back to look and saw Coach Dill's car approaching.

Joe and Mary waited until he parked the car and was heading toward the school before they stopped him. Coach Dill was halfway to the school entrance when he heard Joe calling for him. He stopped and turned.

"Hey, Joe. How's summer vacation going?" he asked.

"It's going okay," he replied.

"What can I do for you?"

"I wanted to ask you about Mary Teller," Joe said.

The question surprised Coach Dill. He was stunned and looked as if he had been smacked across the face.

"What? Why?" the Coach said quickly, as he processed the question.

"I wanted to ask you about Mary," Joe said. "I know she met with Mrs. Johnson and you the day she disappeared. I wanted to ask what the meeting was about."

"How do you know that? And why are you asking?" Coach Dill asked, regaining his composure, and coming back into the conversation. It didn't seem like he was opposed to talking about Mary. It was more like he was expecting a different question and conversation entirely.

"Well, since I found her, I can't get her out of mind, and I've been asking people a lot of questions," Joe said. He wasn't lying. She was in his mind constantly, and the fact that she was standing there listening in on the conversation…yep, not leaving his mind anytime soon, either.

"Oh. So you were the one that found her," he said. "I heard that one of the kids had but didn't know which one. How are you doing? That must have been something."

"Yeah, I am fine. Just trying to figure out what happened to her," Joe said.

"I see. Well, Mrs. Johnson had already told the police everything about that day. But let's see…this happened a long time ago." Coach Dill got quiet, remembering the event. "Yes, I was at school that day and met with Mrs. Johnson. We had an…um…meeting on upcoming sports events that the school newspaper was going to cover. Mary surprised us by arriving early for their meeting."

"Do you remember anything about that day that was different?" Joe asked.

"I remember that there was a storm coming and that Mrs. Johnson told Mary that she better get home before it got bad, so they ended the meeting early," Coach Dill said.

"Hmm…Do you remember her camera?" Joe asked.

"What?"

"Her camera. They never found it. Did she have it with her? I know she was taking pictures with it earlier that day," Joe said.

"Oh…um…no. I don't remember," the coach said.

Mary stood there beside Joe and gasped suddenly at something she just remembered, "Oh my gosh! He took my camera!"

"You took her camera?!" Joe said, half surprised by Mary saying it, but also accusing Coach Dill without thinking.

Coach Dill visibly paled, and took a step back at the accusation. Instead of answering, he kept backing up, looked down at his watch and then behind him, at the doors. "I don't know what you're talking about but…uh…I'm running late for a meeting and I have to go."

Joe, dumbstruck at the sudden turn of the conversation and seeing the retreating form of Coach Dill, quickly regained his train of thought and tried one more time to ask a question. "Coach, why did you take her camera?"

"I'm sorry but I really must go," Coach Dill said, as he got farther away. Joe would have had to yell if he wanted to continue the conversation, but he couldn't, because before he knew it, Coach Dill disappeared behind the doors to the entrance to the school.

"Well, that was weird," Joe said, and then turning to Mary. "What did you remember?"

She looked at him and said, "I don't remember it clearly but as soon as he started talking about Mrs. Johnson telling me to go home, it suddenly all came back to me. I left the meeting and I didn't see Coach Dill until after I left the building. I was about where we are now when he stopped me."

"He stopped you?" Joe said.

"Yes," Mary said. "He did and then asked for my camera, which I gave to him. I thought he was going to give it right back, but then he wouldn't."

"But why would he do that?" Joe questioned.

"I don't know. I asked for it back and he said that he would give it back to me on Monday at school.

I got angry at him and started yelling at him that it was mine and to give it back. He just kept saying that he would give it back on Monday and pretty much did the same thing…he backed off, but I kept right up with him."

"What happened next?"

"He told me that he would talk to Mrs. Johnson about removing me from the school newsletter staff if I continued to protest and that he would call my parents. Then, he told me that I should get on home because the storm was almost here," Mary said.

She then looked as if she were reliving it right there. "I was so angry, I started crying because I didn't understand what I did wrong. He just looked at me and told me to go home. I turned and ran…and then…that's all I can remember. I just remember leaving the school yard and then nothing. I can't remember anything after that."

"That's so weird," Joe said.

"Yeah, it was," Mary said and then continued, "Looks like we are done here for now."

She looked up at the storm brewing and had a thought. "Maybe we can head toward my house and through the woods, where I was found, before that storm hits. It might jog some memories."

"Good idea," Joe agreed.

They left the school yard and headed toward the woods. They didn't see anyone around when they left, but one person had noticed and watched Joe as he walked away. After Joe disappeared from sight, that person followed him.

Chapter Fourteen

The wind kicked up once they entered the wooded area. It was the type of cool breeze that, on a hot day, felt refreshing but you could also detect an energy in the air, which signified something powerful on the way. The trees were swayed slightly and you could hear the wind breathe through them. The rain hadn't hit yet, but it would soon be there. The leaves on the trees turned upside down, displaying the lighter green undersides, apparently waiting for the rain.

"Well, anything?" Joe asked, hopefully.

"It feels the same. I was upset. A storm was coming in and...I wasn't alone. It's...almost there but it's...Nope, it's not there," Mary said.

"That's good, though. It's coming back. Pretty soon, we will know who killed you, Mary," Joe said.

They weren't quite to the spot where Mary's bones had been found, but they were well within the veil of the trees. As they walked the trail, getting closer to that spot, their conversation tapered off, partly because there wasn't much to say at this point and partly to give Mary more time to focus on remembering. As they stopped, they listened to the the wind rush through the trees and it was momentarily peaceful, that is, until they heard something in the woods behind them. It was quiet and had they been talking, they wouldn't have noticed it with the rustling of the trees, but it was there—almost indiscernible movement through the brush. Someone or something was in the woods with them and they couldn't see who or what it was. They immediately looked at each other in alarm. It was hard not to panic and bolt. Joe wasn't sure whether to stay put, run, hide, or walk quietly away. Joe noticed something and had it been any other time, it would have been funny but right now it wasn't. He noticed how time can seem to speed up and slow down, depending on the situation at hand. With all the options that were now flowing through his head, time seemed to slow down, at least enough for him to quickly consider all these options, as well as make this quick observation regarding time. But even though time seemed to be lagging, he was unable to determine the best course of action because fear was setting in. All he knew was that his eyes were probably as big as saucers because Mary's eyes were the same.

The sound of movement got closer, though it was seemingly slower and more deliberate, as if whatever it was, was trying to follow carefully and not alert anyone. The woods and brush were dense in some areas and not in others. Visually, a person in the woods could only see ten to fifteen feet until brush, bush, or tree blocked their view. The sound was creeping closer and a decision had to be made. Joe surveyed the area and saw that there was a group of three bushes, about 3 feet tall, just off the trail that he could hide in. They were clumped closely together and were relatively thick, other than a small space in the middle in which he could conceal himself. He played hide and go seek a bunch of times in these woods and those bushes were one of the best hiding places he had discovered; very rarely was he ever found. Quickly, he made his way inside the safety of the leaves and tried to quiet his breathing. He became more alert to everything around him, with his heightened senses from the adrenaline dump now coursing through his body. He could hear and feel his heartbeat as the blood flowed through and near his ears. It was pounding deep in his chest and he realized he was breathing heavily, so he took a deep breath in an attempt to center his respiration. In the back of his mind, he wondered how he even got here. He thought about his parents. He thought about his friends. He wanted to see them all again. He realized that if he let his imagination go wild with thoughts of what ifs and unknowns, the panic would only build and get worse. He steeled himself and had to actively make the decision to focus. Mary was beside him. She wasn't as worried as he was, since she couldn't be seen, but she was concerned for his safety. Trying to lighten the mood, she smiled and said, "Well at the very least, if something happens, worst case scenario would be that you end up on this side with me."

Joe just looked at her, flabbergasted. Totally not the right thing to say at that moment. He was barely keeping it together. Mary realized as soon as it escaped her lips that it was really poor timing for a quip like that, so she quickly apologized. She was going to explain why she said such a thing, but Joe quickly put his finger to his lips in the universal gesture of "be quiet." He wanted to listen and not be distracted, so he could be ready for anything once whatever it was got to where they were. It wasn't very far off now—just a few more moments and it would be upon them. The anticipation was killing Joe. The wind was really whipping the trees now, and a few drops of rain started to fall. Lightning struck off in the distance.

Then, Joe heard movement just on the other side of the bush he was hiding in. He was so afraid. He remained as still as he possibly could, worried that any movement would alert whatever made the noise. However, even as he hid there, stock-still, his curiosity was strong and he was anxious to know who or what it was. He slowly crouched and peered through a small opening in the branches to try and catch a glimpse. As he did, he almost lost his balance but in regaining it, he snapped a twig at his feet, making noise. The movement on the other side of the bush stopped. Joe closed his eyes at his own stupidity. Why did he move? He could have just asked Mary to step out to see who it was, but the thought hadn't crossed his mind until that twig snapped. As his father always said, hindsight is usually 20/20. He decided to go ahead and get a glimpse of who, or what, was about to discover them and it was...

"ANDREW!"

Chapter Fifteen

"Andrew, what are you doing!?" Joe yelled in surprise, which not only scared Andrew but also Joe himself. It was Andrew, his young friend from the gang, glasses and all. Relief flooded through Joe. He had been afraid that it was someone else like Coach Dill, who he wasn't sure, at this point, whether he was or was not a killer. But the surprise left him going through a whole host of emotions all at once: surprise, relief, anger. Then as a mixture of all three as one gave way to another, Joe felt the weight drop off his chest.

"Joe?!" Andrew said. He was startled at his name being yelled.

"What are you doing?" Joe asked, as he came out from the bushes.

"I could ask the same of you Joe," Andrew replied.

"Were you following us...I mean, me?" Joe said, quickly correcting himself.

"Well no...yes...I mean, Joe, you have been acting weird ever since you touched those bones," Andrew said.

"No, I haven't," Joe said.

"Yes, you have! You haven't really hung out with us since then and even then, when you are around us, you act weird. It's like you are avoiding us. I was heading to the school playground when I saw you walking away earlier. It looked like you were talking to yourself, so, I decided to follow you to see where you went," Andrew said.

"I wasn't talking to myself," Joe said.

"Could have fooled me," Andrew replied.

The rain started to develop a little more in a sprinkle but they could hear the heavier downpour coming.

"Crap, I'm going to get wet and catch a cold," Andrew said, pushing up his glasses. Joe knew where that came from because he had heard Andrew's mom say that to him a thousand times.

"Where is everyone else?" Joe asked.

"Well, like usual, we all were going to meet at the playground but with this storm, maybe they decided not to come," Andrew said. "Anyway I didn't see them when I left to follow you."

Joe was about to reply but the urgency of the storm and rain changed his mind. He told Andrew to follow him to nearby First Baptist Church, because they could find shelter underneath the front porch and wait out the storm. They had to hurry, though, because the storm had arrived and was about to let loose a deluge. They ran as quickly as they could through the woods and across the open ground, toward the church. Fortunately, they made it to the overhang of the front porch just in time, because as soon as they were underneath it, it started pouring. That's the interesting thing about summer storms— they will pop up out of nowhere and be gone before you know it. They can be very strong even if they don't last long. There was no one out on the streets in this weather and no one was at the church except for Andrew and Joe. Well, Mary was there too, but she couldn't be seen so she didn't count.

Breathlessly, they plopped down on the bench that sat near the front door of the church. They had run as hard as they could to avoid getting drenched and it took them a moment to regain their breath.

"That was close," Andrew said, taking his glasses off and using the bottom of his shirt to wipe away the water droplets that had collected, before replacing them on his face.

"Yes, it was," Joe agreed.

The storm looked like it was going to be around for a while, so they settled in and waited. It was coming down in sheets now and wind was buffeting them in their little cove of shelter. Every once in a while, some water would get on them, but not enough to be really worried about.

"So, what's been going on with you Joe?" Andrew asked.

"Nothing," Joe said, but he knew he had to offer some type of explanation because the absence of information just begged for more scrutiny. Andrew was giving him a skeptical, "I don't believe you" type of look, so Joe knew that any explanation was better than nothing. He looked at Mary and she just shrugged her shoulders, offering no advice.

"I don't know Andrew, I...just..." Joe started, as he was thinking of what to say. "I'm trying to figure out what happened to Mary, the girl we found. She is constantly on my mind."

Mary winked and smiled at him with a mischievous grin. "Can't get me off your mind, can you?" she said laughingly.

Joe wanted to respond so badly but had to ignore her as he continued to explain to Andrew. "And since I can't get her out of my mind, it's not that I'm avoiding you" (although he totally was and he knew it). "I'm just deep in thought, trying to figure everything out."

156

That explanation seemed to work as Andrew took it as truth, "That makes sense. So, what have you figured out so far?" Andrew asked.

"I haven't come to any conclusions, really, but I've been going around asking different people about her," Joe said.

"Who have you talked to?" Andrew asked.

"Well, I talked to Mr. Winters, and Coach Dill," Joe began.

"Oh! Coach Dill—I don't like that guy," Andrew said. "He's a creep. He pretends to be nice, but I don't know…there always seems to be an angle with him."

Joe took a moment to think about what Andrew had said. He was surprised at the comment and the insight that Andrew, even being so much younger than him, pointed out. Coach Dill did have that kind of vibe to him. Joe remembered that he did seem to hug the girls a lot and some of the girls didn't like it at all. He would have to ask Mary if he was the same way when she knew him, once they were alone again. He looked at Mary and she was just listening in, making no obvious reaction. He turned back to look at Andrew and continued. "I also talked to the sheriff, and I spoke to Mr. Brown…well, before he died," Joe said.

"Oh! Oh! That's something else I wanted to talk to you about," Andrew said immediately, almost interrupting Joe, as he had just remembered something.

"What?" Joe asked.

"Did you hear about Mr. Brown? They think it was a murder," Andrew said.

"What?" Joe asked. He knew it wasn't suicide but as far as he knew, Mary and he were the only ones that were sure of it. He continued, "What did you hear?"

Mary leaned in with interest, wanting to make sure she could hear. The storm was still raging and although they could hear each other talk, the rain was a bit loud. Joe also leaned in a little closer, to make sure he heard whatever Andrew was about to say. Andrew didn't seem to notice the change in focus and attention from Joe.

"Well, I overheard my mom talking to my aunt Sally and she heard from her friend, who heard from a deputy at the scene or maybe it was a brother of a deputy or...well...I don't know. Anyway, what I heard was that the gun they found didn't have any fingerprints on it, not even Mr. Brown's. So, they think that the killer wiped his fingerprints clean or used gloves, but in their hurry, didn't think to put Mr. Brown's fingers around it. Isn't that wild? We have a killer in town! It could be anyone," Andrew said excitedly about that last bit.

"Well, duh," Mary said, more to herself than anyone else, rolling her eyes.

The rain continued for a bit longer before it lightened up and then stopped altogether. It was getting to be midday and Joe felt his stomach start to rumble, anticipating lunch, and he knew where he would be going next: home. Andrew and Joe talked until the storm let up with Mary just listening in. The conversation shifted from the town's current events to all sorts of other things. Before they left to go their separate ways, Andrew asked if Joe would join them tomorrow, meaning him and the other guys, at the school playground in the morning. It was true that it had been the usual routine; the boys would usually meet up there before going and exploring or whatever else they decided to get into. Joe looked at Mary and then to Andrew. "I'll try and be there," he said.

"That's not an answer," Andrew said. "You either will or you won't. So what is it?"

Mary looked at Joe and said, "You should. It won't bother me. Besides, maybe one of the others may have heard something."

Joe nodded at her and then replied to Andrew, "Ok, I will be there."

"Good," Andrew said.

They said their goodbyes and Joe was alone with Mary again, walking back to his house.

Mary looked at Joe with a smile, as she gently chided him, "You should have seen your face back there in the woods, before you knew it was Andrew."

Joe wanted to respond with a snarky or witty comeback but decided to be truthful instead. "Well, I was scared. I didn't know who it was."

"Well, to be fair, I was scared for you," she said.

"I know! Your eyes were as big as mine were, I'm sure," Joe said.

Mary's smile dropped a little and she explained, "Yeah, the whole thing reminded me of the last moments of my life."

Joe wasn't expecting that and apologized.

"No, it's okay. But it's true. The day I died, there was rain, and it was so similar—the buildup of the fear inside, the scramble to hide and…but I'm no closer to remembering who killed me. That part is gone. It's like Swiss cheese—I remember certain things just fine but then there are these holes that are just…gone," she said. She then sounded more cheerful and hopeful, "But it does seem that eventually it comes back in parts or sometimes even whole memories at a time."

"Oh yeah?"

"Yeah, like when I was first reawakened, I was only vaguely aware of who I was and that something was "off." I was in that ground a long time, unlike Mr. Brown. When I talked to him, it seemed like he was totally himself. It could have been because it was immediately after his death and there wasn't time for his memory to deteriorate. I'm not sure, but I do know that when I read the diary or meet people through you, boatloads of memories come back. It's kinda like one of those big firework displays. You know—when one explodes and it lights up the sky in a big circle of different colors. I mean…I guess that's the best way I can describe it," Mary said.

"So, that's sort of what happened when you saw Coach Dill, huh? It came back to you just like that?" Joe asked.

"Yeah, exactly like that," she said.

"That reminds me," Joe said. "Andrew mentioned something about Coach Dill that made me think about something. Did he ever hug you a lot or act weird around you? Anything out of the ordinary?"

"What do you mean?" she asked.

"I don't know. When Andrew mentioned that he had a weird feeling to him, it reminded me of some stuff I heard from other girls in my class—that he liked to hug them and some of them didn't like it. I've even seen him do it a couple of times. At the time it didn't seem weird, but now, I don't know," Joe said.

"You know, I think I do remember him being a little touchy, but he was like that with all the girls from what I remember. He didn't single anyone out," she said.

"Weird," Joe said.

"Definitely weird," Mary replied.

They arrived back at the house and Joe noticed that his mom's car wasn't in the driveway and the front door was locked. He unlocked it, went inside and walked to the kitchen. His mom had left a note on the counter, saying that she had to run to the store for a few items and would be back shortly. He quickly made a sandwich and ate it.

"You don't ever get hungry?" Joe asked.

"Nope," Mary said. "I mean…I can taste things…and smell. Obviously I can hear. But I'm not hungry… or thirsty, for that matter. I honestly hadn't thought about it until you mentioned it."

Joe heard a car pull up outside and guessed that his mom had come home. She came in a moment or two later. "That storm was something, I'm glad that you weren't out in it," she said as soon as she saw him.

"Yeah, Andrew and I had to seek shelter at the church because we were out walking around when it hit so suddenly."

"I know! I was out driving in it. I couldn't even see the side of the road. It was crazy," she said, then continued, "I'm glad you're home. I want you to stick around the house this afternoon. When your dad gets home from work, we are going to take dinner over to the Teller house. A few of us from church came up with a calendar to get them food for the next couple of weeks. That's why I had to run to the store to grab some extra stuff—so I can prepare a meal to take over. That family must be going through so much right now, with their daughter being found. And not knowing if the death of Mr. Brown is connected to her death or not, must just add to it."

"What are you fixing?" Joe asked.

"Meatloaf," his mom said, as she was navigating the kitchen, getting out what she would need to prepare it. She didn't see the look of momentary disgust on Joe's face. Joe liked most of everything that his mom made but he couldn't stand meatloaf. Someone along the way complimented his mom on it and now, that's her "go to" meal to make whenever there was a function, or potluck, or someone needed food or support.

"Well, I hope they like it," Joe said.

His mom stopped, knowing how he felt about meatloaf, and gave him a look that bordered between irritation and amusement.

"Get out of here and let me cook," she said.

"Will do!" Joe said and left the kitchen, going back to his room with Mary in tow, to wait until his dad got home. When they got to his room, he sat on his bed and Mary sat beside him. He looked at the clock on the nightstand and saw that they had a couple of hours to wait. His dad usually pulled in the driveway around 4:30 p.m.

"So, we are going to your house tonight. How do you feel about that?" Joe asked.

"Nervous," Mary said. "Don't get me wrong—I want to see my family but that quick moment seeing them last time we were there...I just didn't expect the changes and I'm afraid of what else I'll see that I am unprepared for."

"I'll be there with you," Joe said. Or rather, she'd be there with him, he thought to himself, but decided that quip wouldn't be funny right now. Mary looked serious and Joe couldn't bring himself to razz her. So, they just sat quietly for a bit, each deep in their own thoughts and that was okay. It was a moment later that Joe realized that they didn't have to say anything. Just being there next to each other, not saying a word, was just as fine and enjoyable as being silly and filling the silence with banter. But finally Joe did break the silence.

"What did you want to be when you grew up?" Joe asked.

"Hmm...I wanted to be a writer, or a journalist," she replied. "You?"

"A millionaire!" Joe said, laughing.

"Seriously, what do you want to be?" she asked.

He looked at her stone-faced. "Seriously, a millionaire," then broke into a smile and said, "I'm kidding. I don't know. Maybe a police officer. Or a pilot. Something adventurous."

But even as he spoke those words, he was thinking about the adventures he had the past couple of days and now, he wasn't so sure that he really wanted to do something overly adventurous.

"Or maybe, I will just go to school and become a teacher, or something," he said.

"Well, you have plenty of choices and I think you will do fine with whatever you decide. I wish I had the same," Mary said.

Joe immediately felt uncomfortable. It was true—all of Mary's decisions, goals, desires, options—they were gone. Mary noticed and said, "Oh, I don't mean to be a downer. I was just stating the facts and I wish things were different."

"Me too," Joe said.

The afternoon slipped by and Joe's dad pulled into the driveway on time. It took his mom another hour to finish making the meal for the Teller family. Once she was done, they all piled into the family car and headed over. They could have walked, as it was only a couple blocks away. Pretty much everything in this village was only a couple blocks away, but his mom didn't want to carry everything. They pulled up into the driveway and got out.

"Mom, are we going to stay?" Joe asked.

"I don't know. We are dropping this off and if they want us to stay to chat for a bit, we will. It's up to them," his mom replied.

"I don't even want to be here," his dad mumbled and then continued, "I don't know what to say."

"No one does, Harold," his mom replied.

With a sigh, his dad said, "All right, let's do this." He shut off the engine and got out at the same time his mom did. Joe got out and grabbed the food containers with the meatloaf (yuck) that were beside him in the backseat, then followed his parents up to the door. Mary walked beside Joe and her face didn't betray anything she was thinking. Before they got to the front door, it opened, and Mrs. Teller asked them to come on inside. Joe's dad gave him a resigned look that said, "I guess we are going to stay for a bit."

As they walked in, Mr. Teller was sitting in a recliner and got up to greet them.

"Joe, you can go ahead and put the food on the counter in the kitchen," Mrs. Teller said.

Joe knew exactly where the kitchen was, you know, since it wasn't that long ago that he had broken into this house. Even if he had not recently been inside, the house wasn't very big, and he could see the kitchen from the entrance. He walked in and put the food down, then returned to the living room.

"Would you like some tea?" Mrs. Teller asked.

"Sure, I'll come and help you with that," Joe's mom said.

Mr. Teller sat back down in his recliner and Joe's dad sat down on the couch. Joe didn't know what else to do, so he sat beside his dad while his mom and Mrs. Teller had gone into the kitchen to pour glasses of tea for everyone.

Mr. Teller was the quiet sort, so it was a little uncomfortable. His dad didn't know what to say either, so he stayed quiet as well. They could hear the ladies in the kitchen making conversation while they were preparing the drinks. Mary just stood there in the living room, but all of a sudden, without explanation, she walked down the hall and disappeared. Joe was curious but he continued to sit there beside his dad. It would be rude (and strange) to just get up and go exploring. His Mom and Mrs. Teller came back into the room with a tray of glasses of sweet tea for everyone, and placed it on the coffee table in front of the couch. Everyone took a glass and a sip. His mom then sat down on the couch next to Joe and Mrs. Teller sat down in another chair on the other side of the coffee table.

"Thank you so much for coming and bringing food over," Mrs. Teller said.

"Oh, it's our pleasure," Joe's mom replied. "I can't even imagine what you are going through. How are you both holding up?"

"We are taking it a day at a time," Mrs. Teller said. "Sheriff Mattson came by earlier today to check on us and give us an update."

"Oh yeah?" Joe's mom asked.

"Yes, he has been really concerned, especially since the news of Mr. Brown. There is so much going on right now, we were afraid that the town had forgotten about our sweet Mary. The sheriff comforted us by telling us that wasn't the case, and even mentioned how Joe here was going around asking questions," Mrs. Teller said.

Joe perked up at hearing his name and Mrs. Teller continued looking at him this time. "We also heard it was you that found her, and I'm so grateful you did, but I'm sure it must have been a shock. Are you doing okay?"

"Yes, Ma'am," Joe said, and thinking to himself, "But your daughter is currently haunting me, and I have really good conversations with her, so I don't mind." Again, and as usual, when it came to the subject of the relationship that he had with Mary, he decided to keep that to himself. Mary walked back in the room and stood to the side. A few moments later, Mary's younger—now older—sister, Samantha followed her out of the hallway. She said hello to everyone and then told her mom that she was going out. Her mom told her to be careful and she left, walking out the front door. Mary walked over to the front window and watched quietly as her sister got into a red car that was parked on the road in front of their yard, and left. She must have been deep in thought or something because she wasn't even looking at or acknowledging Joe.

Joe's mom asked Mrs. Teller, "How is Samantha taking everything?"

"It's been tough. Well, it's been tough for all of us."

"Did the sheriff say anything else?" his mom continued.

"Not much, but now they are thinking that Mr. Brown wasn't responsible for Mary's disappearance. To be honest, I never thought he did but those rumors, you know. There were some people in town that thought he could have done it, but with his dying yesterday, the sheriff said that he didn't know whether or not there was a connection with finding Mary. He is keeping all his options open and investigating every lead, and told us he would keep us up-to-date on any development."

From there, the conversation drifted to pleasantries and other things. Mary was strangely quiet through it all, though she did give Joe a half-hearted smile from time to time. After about an hour of conversation, it naturally winded down to the point where it was a good time to say goodbye. Joe's dad and Mr. Teller visibly relaxed at this point. The conversation was mainly between Joe's mom and Mrs. Teller, and the men were just kind of waiting for it to be over.

As they were leaving, Joe felt that he had to say something to Mrs. Teller. One, because he knew

Mary would like them to know and two, he knew that Mr. and Mrs. Teller would like to know also. He got Mrs. Teller's attention and said, "Mrs. Teller, I'm pretty sure that wherever Mary is, even after all this time, she wants you to know that she loves you and Mr. Teller very much…and even Samantha, although they weren't close when she disappeared.

Mrs. Teller stepped back, a little shocked, as this was unexpected. She promptly regained her composure, looked at him and said "Thank you, Joe." Mrs. Teller then looked at all of them, smiled meekly and said, "You know, it's really strange. After all this talk about everything and all the events this past weekend, I almost feel as though Mary is right here with us. I know it sounds crazy, but it's true."

Joe thought to himself, "You have no idea how true it is, Mrs. Teller."

"I'm sorry." She continued, "I didn't mean to say that."

"Oh, it's totally all right. We enjoyed the conversation and if you need anything, don't hesitate to call. We'll be right over," Joe's mom said.

They said their goodbyes and Joe's family returned home. When they got there, Joe's dad expressed that he was glad that was over, but admitted he was happy they had all gone. His Mom agreed. Sometimes, it's tough to do the right thing, and this was one of those times—helping others even when it's uncomfortable and you're not exactly sure how to help.

The rest of the evening was pretty uneventful. Joe and his family ate dinner when they got home. Since his mom made meatloaf for the Teller family, she made another batch for them (ugh), which Joe begrudgingly ate. Mary was still keeping to herself and not saying much, which was totally understandable to Joe. She had been through a lot this evening, and Joe knew that she would talk whenever she felt comfortable enough, so he gave her some space. He just had to have patience until then. Mary did say one thing to Joe on the car ride home: "Thanks for telling my family I love them. I miss them so much." Her eyes quietly filled with tears and she remained silent after that.

When Joe got ready for bed and after he told his parents good night, he came into the room and shut the door. Mary was sitting at the small desk, waiting for him, and got up when he came in. Joe looked at her and said, "It's your turn for the bed tonight."

"Ok," she said, then walked over to the bed and lay down. After a few seconds, she propped herself up on one arm to look at Joe and watched as he was preparing a place on the floor to sleep. Before he got too far along, she scooted over to make room and said, "You could sleep on the bed with me. There's plenty of room for the both of us."

"Are you sure?" Joe asked.

A little of the Mary he was used to came shining through, as she looked at him and gave him a wicked smile. "Of course...but don't you get any ideas, young man."

This naturally caused Joe to blush. He had no such ideas but now, he was embarrassed. Mary laughed, but not in a mean way; it was the carefree way that she usually laughed.

"I didn't mean to embarrass you. I was just kidding. But seriously—it's okay. You don't have to sleep on the floor," she said.

Joe, unsure of himself, just said "all right" and got into bed next to her. He reached over to the lamp on the nightstand and turned it off, then laid his head back on his pillow. There was room for the both of them; it was tight, but not uncomfortable. Mary was beside him and he could smell the scent of lavender and feel her warmth as he tried to relax. In the dark, they lay there, then Mary broke the silence.

"That was so hard to go through tonight...at my parents' house."

Joe rolled to his side to look at her. She remained on her back, looking up at the ceiling. With the lamp off, it was dark but there was still a little ambient light coming in from the streetlamp outside.

It was just enough light to allow him to make out her features.

"Do you want to talk about it?" he asked.

"No...yes...I don't know," she responded but continued, "When we got there, I don't know why, but I could feel that my sister was there, so I went looking for her. I wasn't prepared for what I found. My little sister...is now my big little sister. She's all grown up. To me, she is still the little eight-year-old and now all of a sudden, she is an adult. I just wasn't expecting that."

Mary raised her hand to wipe away something from her eye. She wasn't actively crying but Joe guessed that tears were welling up in her eyes, just like they had earlier. He grabbed her other hand and gave it a gentle squeeze. She squeezed back and then rolled to her side to look back at Joe. In the dark, he could barely see her, but she was beautiful to him. Deep inside, whether good or bad, his heart was developing feelings for this girl.

"Thanks for listening," she said.

"Sure—anytime. I'm here for you," Joe said, but felt stupid for saying it because it sounds so cliché. Half the time, he wasn't sure what to say. However, this time it seemed to be the right thing at the right time, because he saw her smile before lying back down to look up at the ceiling.

"I know, and I am glad that you are," she said.

A couple seconds later, she said, "I think tomorrow, I'm going to see if I can write a couple of things in my diary. If that works, once this is all over, would you make sure my family gets it? I just want them to know how much I love them."

"I can do that, but I think they know that you love them," Joe said.

"I know, but I remember my sister and I having a fight before I disappeared. I just want to change that so that it's not her last memory of us together. Maybe by writing something, explaining that I was sorry and was planning to make things better, it will...I don't know," she said.

"I think that's a great idea, Mary. I'll make sure they get it," he said.

"Thanks," she said, then added, "I'm glad you decided to sleep up here with me. It feels good to have you beside me."

Joe felt the same way and said, "Me too."

Silence followed for a couple of minutes before they finally told each other good night and went to sleep.

Chapter Sixteen

The next morning, they woke up and found themselves snuggled up against one another. Joe woke up first and didn't want to move and ruin the moment or what he felt. He remembered what she said about taking things for granted and in the back of his mind, he knew that he better enjoy the moment now, because who knew how long it would last? He kept thinking that he would have really enjoyed her being his girlfriend had they been born about the same time. The past few days had been a whirlwind of emotions and conversations. Joe experienced things he had never experienced before and, as he had noticed before, he felt like he had known Mary a lot longer than the short time since they had met. Then he had a moment of clarity: this is going to hurt when this—whatever this is—was over. But for the time being, he couldn't help himself and Mary wasn't going anywhere, at least not today. Enjoy the moment! Don't think about the future; just enjoy the moment—the "now." But the more he tried to focus, the more he reminded himself of the uncertain future. He would have continued this spiral of thoughts, but Mary woke up and the smile she gave him could only be described as a ray of sunshine. This brought him back to the "now."

It wasn't long before they were both up. Joe went through his morning routine like usual and they were ready to go meet Andrew and whoever else decided to show up that morning, at the school playground.

Before they left, Mary wanted try writing in her diary, with the idea that she had the night before. She asked Joe to hand her a pen and paper to test out her theory. Since she could touch her diary after Joe touched it, she should be able to do the same with other objects. Joe dug into his school backpack that had been sitting in the corner of his room, untouched, since the last day of this past school year. He pulled out a pen and sheet of paper from a notebook, then walked back over to Mary. Just like with the diary, he handed it to her and she was able to take it! The excitement in her face was contagious and Joe felt excited too! It was like a win on some level but the test wasn't over yet; they still needed to see if she could write. She took the pen and paper, sat down at the small desk and began writing. Sure enough, words crafted with a concise, yet beautiful, penmanship that Joe could only dream of, flowed across the paper. It actually worked out! Being able to follow through and at least salvage something from her life was momentous and the feeling matched. She was both relieved and excited. She quickly put the paper to the side and grabbed her diary. She then took a few minutes to furiously write, taking a moment every now and then to stop and think about what she wanted to say to her big little sister. Then as quickly as she had started, she finished. With a satisfied smile, she put the diary away in her jacket.

"Ok, now I'm ready. We can go," Mary said.

"Are you sure you want to go hang out with the gang?" Joe asked.

"Sure. Why not? They're your friends," Mary said.

"Right, but won't you be bored? It's not like we will be able to talk," Joe said.

"Do you think I only revolve around you?" Mary said.

"Uh...no. That's not what I meant," Joe said.

"Just because you're the only one who can see me, it doesn't mean I need you to entertain me."

"I know that. I was just..." Joe attempted to talk but Mary cut him off. She continued to pester him with points of why he doesn't need to worry about her, before she broke off in a smirk that let Joe know she was completely messing with him. Just another reason why he liked her—she was unpredictable but in a good-natured way that he felt comfortable with.

"I'm just kidding," she said as she touched his shoulder. "I know what you were trying to do. It's okay. I don't mind hanging out. Besides, you really shouldn't ignore your friends on my account."

Joe relaxed and was glad she understood. He was really only thinking of her. He knew that if roles were reversed, he wasn't sure he'd like to be a tagalong without even being part of the group. He couldn't even imagine how that must feel, but at the same time, he kind of did. He thought back on uncomfortable situations in which he was either surrounded by girls he couldn't bring himself to talk to, or around others that he wanted to impress but didn't know what to say, so he just clammed up. In poor Mary's case, she couldn't talk to anyone even if she wanted to, whereas when he'd been in those situations, he totally could have had he chosen to. He just didn't want her to be alone in her thoughts long enough to dwell on her losses and feel sad.

"Ok, I just wanted to make sure," Joe said.

They left Joe's room and, on the way out, Joe made a quick detour to tell his mom where he was heading, grab a granola bar and out the door they went, he and Mary. It was a sunny day and it felt really nice out. The breeze was cool and there wasn't a cloud in the sky except for the really thin, swirly ones that looked like spirits because they were so far away in the atmosphere.

As Mary and Joe were walking, they were also chatting, bantering back and forth, and goofing around. As they came to the next crossroad on their way to the school yard, Joe thought about Mr. Brown. This would be the road they could turn on to go to the store, if they wanted to. Joe looked down the street toward Mr. Brown's store. Yep, just a couple blocks that way and it's right there.

"It's weird," Joe said. "Although I know Mr. Brown's store is closed, I still have that idea that, 'Oh, I will just stop by the store for a Coke,' or 'I will go play that video game there,' but it's not an option anymore. Funny how we get conditioned to do things."

"Yeah, change is weird. Takes a bit to get used to it. I know all about it," Mary said.

Joe looked at her and thought, "I bet she does." They continued forward and arrived at the playground. Andrew was already there. Most of the time, but not the case yesterday, he was the first one to arrive, since he lived closest to the school—just a few houses down.

Coach Dill's car was in its usual parking space, so he had already arrived at the school. Joe greeted Andrew and Andrew responded, surprised, "You came! I really thought you'd be a no-show."

"Ye of little faith," Joe jokingly responded, but knew that Andrew was right. He really had no intentions of coming this morning. Had Mary suggested anything else, they would have done something different. It wasn't long before Matt showed up, along with brothers Johnny and Frankie, and they all expressed their disbelief that Joe was there.

"He's alive!" Frankie said, laughing.

"And he decided to join us," Johnny followed.

Matt just said "Hey" and didn't join in on making fun of Joe. In the grand scheme of their friendship, this wasn't near as bad as it could have been. It was just a light ribbing, welcoming him back into the group since he had atypically been absent the past couple of days. The last several days had been very atypical for the whole town, so amends had to be made. Nothing was as it should be, so they didn't give Joe too much of a hard time.

"So, how are you feeling Joe?" Matt asked.

"All better?" Frankie asked.

"I'm good," Joe replied.

"You sure?" Johnny said, "You have been acting weird since we found those bones."

"Yep," Joe said. "I know…you've all told me, at different times, how weird I've been, but I'm okay now."

He really wanted to tell his friends about everything that had happened but felt that this was one of those things they just wouldn't understand. That—and this was something special that he shared only with Mary, and he sort of wanted to keep it that way.

So, to change the subject, Joe asked, "What's the plan today?"

"Well, we can't go to the gas station," Frankie said.

"We could go back out to the cemetery," Andrew said. "We had a good time the other day, but you weren't with us, Joe."

As they discussed ideas and different plans for the day, two sheriff cruisers came speeding up the road, causing the boys to immediately stop talking and pay attention to what was unfolding in front of them. The cruisers turned into the school parking lot and stopped near the door. Sheriff Mattson got out of one cruiser and a deputy got out of the other. They both met up in front of the doors to the school and went in. They looked serious and like they meant business about whatever it was that was waiting for them inside.

Joe had heard a door shut and looked around. It didn't come from the school but from one of the houses nearby. The other kids were too transfixed by the developments at the school to notice. He wasn't sure but thought maybe it had come from Mr. Daniels' house. He couldn't figure it out but when he was about to turn back toward the school, he thought he saw the curtain in the front window of Mr. Daniels' house move, ever so slightly…but it could have been his imagination, Joe thought. He wasn't quite sure, just like he wasn't quite sure where the sound of a closing door had come from. His attention was then brought back toward the school with the chatter of his friends.

"Woah—what do you think that's about?" Andrew said.

"I don't know, but they looked serious," Johnny said.

Joe looked back at the school. He, too, wondered what was going on in the school. Just what had brought the police there this morning? Then an idea formed, and he looked toward Mary and said out loud, "I wish we could find out what they are doing. Too bad we can't go in there without being seen."

He had really emphasized that last part which only brought looks of, "Well, duh" from his friends but Mary nodded thoughtfully and said, "Good idea."

The playground was not very far from the front doors of the school and it only took Mary a few seconds to follow and enter the school, behind the law enforcement officers. When she walked through the front door, she stood in a hallway that stretched the length of the building, with a couple of intersections where hallways crossed. One hallway lead to the gymnasium/ basketball court, which was also used as a makeshift auditorium for other types of school functions, including pep rallies and school theater productions. The hallway walls were two-toned green, with light green plaster on the top half and a darker green wainscoting covering the lower half. The floor had thin, light brown, indoor/outdoor-style carpet. It had a worn and faded look to it after many years of use, but it was clean. She was immediately overcome with the smell from the dusty hallway, which reminded her of old books. With that, it brought back her own memories of the times she spent at the school. Her old locker was right down the hall to the right; she even remembered her old locker combination. Another memory poked through the fog—right in front of the lunchroom door, she had gotten into a fight with an old friend named Clarissa Thompson. They yelled at each other and stormed off in different directions; she couldn't remember what the argument was about. She immediately wondered happened to her, but then snapped out of it and remembered why she was there. She continued walking until she heard voices coming from the teachers' office hallway, which was lined by teachers' offices on each side and ended at the teachers' lounge. It was the only hallway that wasn't frequented by students.

Outside, the gang was still speculating on what was going on, when Joe heard the same sound of a door closing and looked around for the source. He saw Mr. Daniels leave his house and walk toward the school. It didn't take very long before he, too, disappeared behind the doors that Mary had entered just moments before. Joe didn't think much of it, as it was Mr. Daniels' job to keep the school clean. He was just going about his day.

As Mary started down the hall, the voices were muffled, but as she continued, she was eventually able to clearly make out the conversation. "What are you doing here, Sheriff?" Mary heard Coach Dill ask.

"We have a search warrant that was signed by the judge this morning. We need to search your office," Sheriff Mattson said.

"What!? Why?" Coach Dill exclaimed.

Mary walked into the Coach Dill's office and stood to the side, so she could have good vantage point of everyone in the room. It had the same color scheme and carpet as the halls. There were two doors that entered into this office—one that came in from the hallway that Mary just entered from, and another that opened into a smaller hallway that lead to the gymnasium, as well as the boys' and girls' locker rooms. Pictures and certificates adorned the walls— everything from family photos to framed awards he had collected over the years. It was a cozy office with a desk and two chairs for parent/teacher meetings, as well as couple of lockers and file cabinets. Coach Dill was sitting behind his desk, looking up at the sheriff. He looked surprised, but not overly flustered; it was more along the lines of being unexpectedly interrupted, but nothing out of the ordinary. The sheriff looked like a hawk staring at some sort of prey. The deputy had a blank face, devoid of emotion, and Mary surmised that he was there for backup in case this got out of hand. Something was going on here, Mary thought—something very serious.

"We have reason to believe that there might be an item here that could help answer a lot of questions," the sheriff said.

Totally flabbergasted, Coach Dill was trying to process what was going on and failing miserably. "What are you talking about?"

"We received a phone call that there was something in this office that shouldn't be. Do you have any idea or thought as to what it might be?" Sheriff Mattson asked, hoping that he would just confess. Sometimes, a guilty conscience will cause a person to come clean on just about anything. The sheriff hoped that Coach Dill would be the kind of person who would respond in such a way.

"I have no idea what you are going on about, Sheriff," Coach Dill said.

Oh well—I guess we will have to play this thing out, the sheriff thought to himself.

"All right…well…if you wouldn't mind standing up and getting out of the way, we are going to search your office," the sheriff said.

Coach Dill got up and was still not quite sure what was going on. "Sheriff, if you just tell me what this is all about, surely I can help you."

"It's about the Teller girl. Please stand over there," Sheriff Mattson said, as he pointed to the side of the room near Mary.

"What?! What about her?" Coach Dill said, as he got up and moved to the side. He visibly paled and stuttered, "I...I...don't know anything about what happened to her."

The sheriff nodded toward the deputy to start searching while he kept his eye on Coach Dill. "I'm sure it's all just a big misunderstanding, then, but let us look and we'll see what we find."

The deputy rifled through Coach Dill's file cabinets before moving to the lockers. He was very thorough as he moved through each area, taking things out, flipping through files, looking into boxes inside the lockers. He wasted no time as he systematically finished different areas of search. As he did so, the Sheriff and Coach Dill continued to talk.

"What are you looking for?" Coach Dill asked. The initial shock of hearing that the search pertained to Mary was starting to subside, so the color was returning to his face and he was regaining control of his speech. However, there was a slight bead of sweat starting to form across his forehead.

"Well, I was hoping you could tell us. It would really save us time but, we have all day if need be," the sheriff replied.

The deputy finished with the lockers and moved to Coach Dill's desk. He started at the bottom, right drawer. Opening it and peering in, he was about to go delving in but stopped short, then looked at the sheriff and said, "Boss?"

The sheriff came over and looked into the drawer. "I guess the person who called this in was correct. It is here," Sheriff Mattson said. Coach Dill watched them both as the sheriff bent over to retrieve the item and place it on the desk. It was an old film camera that looked well-worn and used, but still functional. Mary knew that camera. As soon as she saw it, she knew it was hers. She had spent plenty of time with it and knew it quite intimately. She remembered that she had to be careful with the latch that held the film canister in place because it was very loose. More than once, she had lost film to an accidental overexposure, because she didn't make sure the latch was in place. It even had her initials "M.T." written on the bottom in permanent marker; it was faded, but anyone could still make them out.

The sheriff looked up from the camera and glared at Coach Dill, "Care to explain this?"

Immediately, Coach Dill lost his color again and turned a light shade of grey. He also stuttered again as he tried to speak. "I...I...don't know where that came from."

"Are you sure?" the sheriff asked. "Because what I got is a little girl dead—missing after coming to school that morning—and you failing to mention this (indicating the camera). With Mr. Brown dead, I could totally see how killing him might have thrown us off the trail, with the stories that were floating around about him."

"What? I didn't kill Mr. Brown and I didn't kill that girl either!" Coach Dill yelled.

"Well, how did this camera get here, then?" the sheriff asked.

"I don't know," Coach Dill said.

"Listen—I am going to arrest you for murder if you don't start talking or making some sense of all this," the sheriff said.

The sheriff picked up the camera, and as he did so, the film door came open and out popped an intact roll of film, falling out onto the desk. He looked at it then back to the Coach. "Well, what do you think is on that roll of film, Coach?" But before Coach Dill could answer, the sheriff commanded, "Now sit down and start talking."

Coach Dill sat down at one of the two chairs he usually reserved for parents or students that came to see him, but his eyes remained fixed on the roll of film lying on his desk. He started to say something, but was interrupted by the sheriff demanding the truth, not whatever was about to come out of his mouth. That threw the coach off. He was bewildered and was planning on saying something—anything—but as the tension rose in the room, and he was the focus of two big and capable men with guns, he felt trapped. It was like the room was closing in on him with no escape. He was so nervous and on the verge of panic. He feared he would lose consciousness but instead, inhaled deeply in an attempt to regain control. He figured the best course of action was to try to explain what he did remember about that fateful day.

"Sheriff, I have done some bad things in my life, but I have never hurt or killed anyone," he said.

"Okay, keep going," Sheriff Mattson replied.

"I did take Mary's camera the day she disappeared, but honest to God, I have no idea what happened to her. I was planning on giving it back to her the following Monday, but the camera was gone when I came back to school Monday morning. Of course, by that time I had heard that she disappeared, but..."

"But what?"

"Well, we didn't know what happened to her and since I couldn't find the camera, I didn't want to be under suspicion or be the subject of interrogation, so I kept it to myself."

"Why did you take her camera?" Sheriff Mattson asked.

"I...uh...that's complicated, Sheriff," Coach Dill replied.

"We aren't going anywhere," he replied, then continued, "What's on that roll of film that has got you so flustered right now? Is that why you took her camera?"

Coach Dill looked down at his shoes and gave a sigh of resignation. "Let me explain. I had just started working here that year. It was my first teaching job and I was thankful to have it. I was a young man with a young wife. We had just had our first child."

"Go on..." the sheriff prompted.

"Well, Mrs. Johnson and I...got really close during my time here," he said. "She wasn't happy with her relationship with her husband and my wife and I were having problems, so she and I...kind of...got together."

"You were having an affair?" the sheriff asked.

"Yes. And we met that day to...uh...fool around before her meeting with Mary. But Mary showed up earlier than expected and surprised us. We were near the window in Mrs. Johnson's office that overlooks the schoolyard. I saw Mary snapping pictures outside and I was worried that it might have shown us in the window in a...uh...compromising position."

"So, that's why you took the camera? To get rid of the film?"

"Yes. After Mary left her meeting with Mrs. Johnson, I caught up with her at the playground and asked for her camera. I told her that I would give it back to her Monday. I then brought it in and put it in my desk, but when I arrived Monday morning, it was gone."

"Why didn't you bring this up when you were questioned all those years ago?"

"I didn't want to lose everything."

"What?"

"Had it gotten out that Mrs. Johnson and I were having an affair, I would have lost my job. My wife would have left me. With a black spot like that on my record, I would have had a hard time finding another job at any other school, so I didn't say anything. I didn't want to have to answer more questions that would have exposed us. Then after a while, the incident with the camera just didn't seem that important."

Coach Dill was sweating profusely now, but at the same time, looked relieved. He took a moment to wipe the sweat from his forehead before continuing.

"At any rate, Mrs. Johnson felt horrible about Mary's disappearance. She blamed herself because she thought if she hadn't sent her home with the storm coming, maybe she wouldn't have disappeared. Of course, the guilt from that ended our relationship. She and her husband divorced a few months later, then she moved away. The whole thing scared me so badly, I never cheated on my wife again."

"Hmm..." Sheriff Mattson said while pondering everything that Coach Dill just said.

The coach, now that he was on a roll, just kept talking. "And this is the first time I have seen that camera since the day I put it there. I haven't seen it since and honestly, hadn't thought about it in a very long time...that is, until yesterday when that boy Joe Anderson asked me about it. I have no idea how he knew anything about the camera. Is he the one who called you?" Coach Dill asked.

The Sheriff peered back at Coach Dill. "I am not at liberty to say who called, but you said that boy showed up and asked you about it?"

"Yes. He stopped me yesterday morning to ask me about Mary, the meeting that she and Mrs. Johnston had, and then he accused me of taking the camera. I was shocked because no one else could have known about it, and it's been so long," Coach Dill said.

"We still need to take you down to the station for more questions and we are going to find out what's on the roll of film," Sheriff Mattson said.

The boys saw the sheriff come out of the front door of the school, carrying something in his hands. When they set out this morning, they certainly didn't expect to witness what was unfolding before them. The deputy followed, bringing Coach Dill out in handcuffs and proceeded to place him in the back of his marked cruiser. He drove off, leaving the sheriff behind. The sheriff walked over to his car and put the object he was carrying in the back seat. He was about to get into the driver's seat, but then noticed the boys at the playground and decided to walk over.

"Joe!" he called, when he was halfway to the group. He motioned for Joe to come meet him.

The boys' excitement immediately dropped as they looked at one another and then to Joe. What could he possibly want with him? They instantly became worried, Joe most of all. Even though the sheriff was his dad's friend, right now he looked like he was on a mission and there was nothing friendly about him.

Joe left his friends behind, murmuring to themselves about Coach Dill, the sheriff and Joe. Joe, not knowing what transpired inside the school, didn't know what any of this was about and slowly walked out to meet the sheriff. The sheriff watched him as he got closer, then saw the other boys talking behind Joe's back, so he yelled at the other boys, "The show is over! Go home now!"

They didn't protest, and reluctantly gathered their stuff. It didn't take very long but they left, leaving Joe behind with the sheriff. They yelled to Joe, to come to Andrew's house when he was done. The sheriff waited for them to be out of earshot, then turned toward Joe to start the conversation.

"Yes sir?" Joe asked

"Did you accuse Coach Dill of having Mary Teller's camera?" Sheriff Mattson asked.

"He had it?" Joe asked. He was, indeed, avoiding the question, partly because he couldn't remember exactly how the conversation went and partly because his curiosity was piqued.

"How did you know he had it?"

"I didn't but…uh…I guessed he might have had it," Joe answered.

"I told you the other day not to go around asking questions. Don't you know it could be dangerous?" the sheriff asked.

"I couldn't help it. I have to find out what happened to Mary," Joe said.

He said it with such conviction that the sheriff was taken aback and now looking at him in a different light. This wasn't just the typical curiosity of a boy; this was different. There was a finality to the statement that, sure enough, this kid wouldn't stop asking questions until he found the answer.

"I think we may have found her killer," the sheriff said.

"You think it's Coach Dill?" Joe asked.

"Possibly. It certainly looks like that could be the case."

"What makes you think that?" Joe asked.

The sheriff was a busy man and he really needed to get to his office to follow up with Coach Dill. He was on the verge of cutting it short and leaving, but due to the seriousness of Joe's attention, he decided to humor him. "He had motive, and he had opportunity. He also didn't speak up about that camera until it was found. That leaves a lot of suspicion in our minds."

Joe agreed, "I guess it could have been him."

Joe couldn't wait to talk to Mary to see what happened inside. Speaking of which, where was she? She hadn't come back outside yet, and Joe started to get concerned. This was the longest they had been apart since they met and he sensed something could be wrong. She should have been back out here by now.

"You okay?" the sheriff asked, noticing his shift in focus.

"Yes sir. Just something on my mind."

He looked at Joe a moment longer and said, "All right, get on to your friends. I'm sure they're waiting on you."

The sheriff turned, indicating that the conversation was over, and walked back to his cruiser. Joe stood there a bit longer and started walking slowly toward the road to make it look like he was leaving, but he wasn't going to go anywhere until he found out what happened to Mary. The sheriff got in his car, rolled down the window and waved to Joe as he left. Once he was out of sight, Joe turned around and headed back toward the front door of the school. He looked around and realized he was alone. There was no one outside that he could see and that made him feel a little uncomfortable. He pushed open the door and went inside. The place seemed strangely empty, especially with his memories of the hallways being full of people during the school year, but that wasn't the case today. He didn't want to go down the hallway yelling Mary's name. Who knew who else could be here that he didn't know about? He decided to slowly walk around and look for her. He figured the best place to look first would be Coach Dill's office, since he had come out with the deputy who Mary had followed in.

The door to Coach dill's office was closed but he could hear crying from inside. He crept closer and thankfully, the door was unlocked when he tried it. He opened the door slightly and saw Mary sitting on the floor next to the desk, visibly upset. Her arms were wrapped around her knees and she was shaking. Shocked at what he found, Joe came in quickly and sat down beside her.

"Mary—what's wrong?" he asked.

She had been rocking back and forth. Her face was red from emotion and she looked at him, tears streaming down her face. Strangely, even though she was upset, he still found her beautiful, but what she said next chilled him to the bone. Her voice was weak but the words she spoke were very clear.

"I know who killed me."

Chapter Seventeen

Joe reached out to her and brought her into a hug that she returned. "Are you okay?" he asked.

So many questions were running through his head, but he didn't want to pepper her with them, overwhelming her more than she already was. She seemed so vulnerable, and with that in mind, he had asked the most important one first. Their embrace and Joe's efforts to console her lasted a few more seconds. She finally pulled away and regained some of her composure, at least enough to say that she was fine. She went on to explain that when all the memories came rushing back at once, it was overpowering.

"Thanks for coming and looking for me," Mary said.

"Of course," Joe replied. "I was getting worried when you didn't return after Coach Dill left with the deputy."

She looked at him and gave him a weak but sweet smile that spoke volumes of gratitude. He smiled back, then stood up and helped her to her feet.

Her face was still red and her eyes puffy, but she was beginning to recover. Then her look changed to alarm as something crossed her mind.

"We need to get out of here," she said.

"What? Why?" Joe asked.

"This isn't a safe place," she said with urgency. "Listen, I will explain everything, but you need to get out of here first."

Joe was confused by the sudden change in her demeanor and focus.

"Oh, come on. It will be all right," Joe said.

"No! You don't understand. You're in danger!" she said forcefully, then grabbed him by the hand to pull him closer toward the door. "We have to be careful and try not to be seen or heard."

"They've already arrested Coach Dill. I think we're safe," Joe protested.

"It wasn't him. It was…" Mary began, but was interrupted by the door swinging open, startling both Joe and Mary.

Mr. Daniels, the janitor and groundskeeper, came walking in, and stood near the doorway. He stopped and looked at Joe curiously but also pointedly. "What are you doing here? And who were you talking to?"

The unexpected appearance of Mr. Daniels surprised Joe. He wasn't expecting him or anyone else to be there. Joe responded, "Uh…nobody." And thinking quickly added, "I was supposed to have a meeting with Coach Dill, but he isn't here."

He quickly stole a glance at Mary who stood stock-still, her face pale from fear, Joe assumed. He found this odd, since her face had been flushed just moments ago. She looked like she was going to be sick…but then her face twisted in rage and she started yelling at Mr. Daniels, who, of course, couldn't hear her.

"You did it, you sick bastard! You killed me. You tried to rape me and then you killed me!" She continued on with other insults and accusations but unfortunately, it fell on deaf ears except for Joe's. Mary was so full of rage that Joe could feel the heat emanating off of her. The newly-revealed truth washed over Joe like a wave of enlightenment and disgust all at once. His face and body must have displayed this revelation, because when he turned back toward Mr. Daniels, the look in his eyes changed from curiosity and narrowed down on Joe. Joe instinctively backed up. Mr. Daniels blocked the doorway to the main hallway, but there was still the other door that led to the back hall and gymnasium.

"What's wrong?" Mr. Daniels asked, stepping forward.

"Nothing," Joe said, taking another step back.

"Something changed. You're looking at me differently. You seem suspicious...or scared."

By this time, Mary had quit screaming but was still watching Mr. Daniels through a face that Joe never wanted to be on the other end of. "If looks could kill," he thought to himself, he wouldn't have to worry about Mr. Daniels anymore.

"You know, Joe," Mr. Daniels started, "I know you've been asking a lot of questions lately. This is a small town and news travels fast."

Mr. Daniels continued to inch forward and Joe kept inching closer to the other door, ready to bolt at any moment. Mr. Daniels continued, "You know, don't you?"

Joe's mind was full of racing thoughts and he instinctively replied, "I have no idea what you're talking about or what you did to Mary."

Immediately after the words escaped his lips, he knew he should have more carefully chosen his reply, in order to sound more convincing. Mr. Daniels now knew that Joe knew, and his eyes narrowed even more, as he moved forward, snarling.

Mary yelled at Joe to run, but he was already moving as soon as he saw Mr. Daniels lunge toward him. He got through the first door with his pursuer close behind. Joe's heart jumped up in his throat as he felt the blood coursing through his body while he was running. He didn't have time to be scared; he only had time to think of an escape. He heard Mr. Daniels behind him, coming through the door that he had just exited. Joe headed through the second door that led into the gymnasium. If he could just make it to the door on the other side of the basketball court, which led to the exterior of the building, he would be home free. Joe heard the second door fling open behind him and the steps get closer. When Joe reached the other side of the court, he had to slow down to push the crash bar so the door would open. The door sprung open and he was halfway through, one foot out the door. Safety was now within reach. As his second foot breached the threshold, he felt hands grab his shoulders and pull him back inside.

The door crashed back on Mr. Daniels, causing him to lose his footing, which, in turn, caused him to lose his grip on Joe's shoulders. He was still very close and remained in front of the door through which Joe had planned his escape. Joe had to think quickly. He decided the only feasible option to evade Mr. Daniels was to run up the bleachers on the side of the room. He hoped that by doing so, he could outrun Mr. Daniels and stay away from him long enough to get back down and out the door. He quickly ran up to the top, but Mr. Daniels was right behind him. Adrenaline was pumping through both of their bodies and although Joe was fast, Mr. Daniels cornered him up at the top of bleachers.

Mr. Daniels was breathing heavily. "I wanna know how you know," he said, as he closed the gap. Joe had no means of escape and couldn't think of anything else to do, so he decided to go all-in and run full-force into Mr. Daniels. He crashed into him and they both went down. This took his assailant off guard, so Joe scrambled to get back up to his feet and continue his way down the bleachers. But Mr. Daniels clawed at Joe's ankles and latched on, bringing him back down. Joe rolled over to his back and was trying to scoot away, but Mr. Daniels had a death grip and pulled him closer. He jumped on top of Joe, wrapped his hands around his throat and began to squeeze. Joe couldn't believe what was happening. This was not, at all, how he thought today was going to go. He could smell Mr. Daniels' aftershave and sweat. It's strange what one notices as they are in the final moments of their life, he thought to himself. He thought about the events of his life, his friends, his family, what he had hoped for the future, wishing that he had more time. Finally, he thought of Mary. Well, at least she will be there waiting for me, he thought.

But Mary was already there. She had followed and watched everything—from Joe's near escape, to the quick tussle at the top of the bleachers, to Mr. Daniels strangling Joe. Joe turned and saw Mary standing beside him. She still looked like an angel to him. But that look of an innocent angel quickly turned to the look of an angel of vengeance, as Mary's face contorted in utter hatred for Mr. Daniels. Joe was about to lose consciousness, but he saw Mary step back, wind her foot back, then start forward to gain momentum before kicking Mr. Daniels in the face. The force of the blow caused him to lose his grip on Joe's throat and the sweet flow of oxygen again seeped back into Joe's lungs, as he lay there, gulping for air.

The look on Mr. Daniels' face was one of absolute confusion. He had no idea where the blow had come from. Mary just stood there, wide-eyed and shocked that it had actually worked. She gambled on the fact that everything Joe touched, she could also touch, so when Mr. Daniels touched Joe, she figured it couldn't hurt to try. Now that she knew that it worked and she could actually touch him, she continued to unleash her anger. Mr. Daniels was on his knees, now looking around, when Mary punched him in the face. Now, it was Mr. Daniels' turn to back away—from an attacker that he couldn't see. This gave Joe the freedom of movement to scoot further away, eventually getting to his feet, as he watched Mary attacking her killer. Mary didn't stop with one punch. She continued to pummel him as he cowered and attempted to stand, all the while trying to protect himself from unseen blows. As he stood, he offered another target which Mary was more than happy to utilize. She delivered a strong kick to the groin, which caused Mr. Daniels to gasp and double over. As he did so, he teetered on the edge of the bleachers' stairs. Mary pushed him, causing him to tumble backwards. With the momentum of the push and Mr.

Daniels' own weight, he crashed end over end, as he went down the full length of the bleachers. He came to a complete stop on the floor and lay motionless.

Joe looked down at Mr. Daniels, then back at Mary, who seemed just as stunned as he was, over what had just transpired. She looked back at Joe and matter-of-factly said, "I think I killed him."

"I think it's okay. He was about to kill me."

"Oh—I don't care about that. He killed me, and he totally deserved this." Then, realizing what she said, she continued, "I mean…I care and I'm glad that he didn't kill you too, but I'm not worried about killing him—at all."

Joe didn't want to, but he made his way down the bleachers to see if Mr. Daniels was breathing. As he got closer, he realized he didn't have to check for breathing after all, because Mr. Daniels' face was pointed in the direction opposite his body. He evidently broke his neck in the tumble down the bleachers.

"Well…now what?" Joe said.

"I have an idea," Mary said, pulling her diary out of the pocket of her jean jacket. She placed it in the one of the larger pockets on Mr. Daniels' uniform, then turned to Joe. "That way, my diary and the messages I left for my family will get to them. It'll also point to him as my killer."

208

"That makes sense. I need to find a phone and call the police," Joe said.

"Yeah, that's a good idea. We need to get out of here because I don't want to be around if he has an afterlife like Mr. Brown did," Mary said.

"I hadn't even thought of that," Joe said, with that thought giving him shivers.

There was a phone near the front of the school that Joe used to dial 911. While they waited, Mary told Joe about her memories of what had happened the day she disappeared. It was true that Coach Dill had taken her camera and she was upset. There was a storm and she was on her way home when Mr. Daniels approached her about making sure she got home safely. She thought that was weird; she wondered why a guy in his mid-twenties was talking to her. She had always thought he was a little strange, but she didn't think much of it. He told her he saw Coach Dill take her camera and said he could get it back for her, but he wanted to make sure she was okay. He wanted to tell her why he thought he had taken her camera. She was curious, so she let him walk with her.

She then told Joe about how, when they got closer to the woods, Mr. Daniels' demeanor changed. He got uncomfortably close and tried to put his arm around her, which scared her. He then became more aggressive and tried to grab a hold of her, saying that

209

she knew that she was interested in him, but she wasn't. He dragged her deeper into the woods and tried to force himself on her, but she slipped away, running. He followed her and caught up to her. He grabbed her again and said not to say anything to anyone. He said that he was sorry, and that it had been a misunderstanding. She started to struggle to get away from him again, and managed to free herself, but when she turned, she tripped and hit her head on a rock that made her woozy. She remembered how the blood started gushing down the side of her head and the pain almost blinded her. She then remembered how he got on top of her, repeatedly saying "sorry" as he strangled her. He said he couldn't allow her to tell anyone what happened. Mary guessed that as soon as she hit her head, he figured he couldn't hide what he did, so decided to kill her and make sure no one could ask questions.

"Wow! This whole time, it was him trying to throw everyone off," Joe said.

They heard sirens in the distance and shortly thereafter, Sheriff Mattson arrived with two deputies close behind. When he saw Joe, his faced tightened and asked, "Are you okay, son? What happened here? Dispatch said that Mr. Daniels tried to kill you and now he is dead? What is this all about?"

By this time, the redness and bruises from the attack were clearly visible on Joe's skin, especially around his neck. Joe explained to the sheriff that after he had left earlier, for whatever reason, Mr. Daniels called him inside and wanted to talk to him about all the questions he had been asking about the Teller girl. After a brief conversation, he began chasing Joe and ultimately attacked him, thinking that he had found out that he was responsible for the girl's disappearance. Joe was luckily able to overpower him and he fell down the bleachers, to his death. It was a little untrue in how it all unfolded but…it was the truth overall. Mr. Daniels was responsible for Mary's disappearance and death. Later, when they found Mary's diary on him, it all but confirmed it for everyone.

Chapter Eighteen

Later that evening, when all the excitement died down and Joe was back home, his parents were fussing all over him because they were so grateful he was not seriously hurt. They were pretty upset, however, that he had put himself in danger and told him to never do anything like that again. Joe was in total agreement with this; he didn't want anything like that to happen to him again, either. Mary disappeared for a time while Joe dealt with his parents but eventually, he was able to get away and returned to his room.

When he walked into his room, he could sense a difference, but was unable to pinpoint what it was. Something was just "off." Mary was waiting for him, sitting at his desk. She smiled as he entered the room. "Well, we did it! We found out what happened to me," she said.

"Yep. We sure did. We make a great team," he said.

"Joe?" she said.

Joe looked at her and immediately, knew what was coming. He didn't want to voice it, as if saying something would make it happen faster. Tears started to come to his eyes, though he tried to hide it. He wished so badly that they wouldn't show. Mary couldn't help but notice and at that moment, she knew that Joe knew what was happening.

"It's time for me to go," she said.

Joe choked up and couldn't say anything. He knew this would happen. He always knew this would end but he had gotten to know her so well.

"Believe me, I wish things were different, too," Mary said, as if she could read his thoughts.

Joe wanted to say so much but was overcome with emotion. And really, what was there to say? "Don't go?" "Stay?" As if any of that would work. Her time was done. Her mission was complete. It was time for her to move on—he knew it. Even though the time had been short, and they had only known each other a few days, she was his best friend and he loved her. He knew that on some level, she loved him too.

"I'm going to miss you," she continued.

He managed to squeak out, "I'm going to miss you too."

214

She stood up and came over to him. She looked him deep in the eyes and gave him a hug. He wrapped his arms around her and hugged her right back. They clung to each other firmly and intentionally; it was the kind of hug that comforted and the kind of hug that evoked a feeling of unmatched closeness. She stepped back. As Joe looked at her, she got a distant look in her eyes as she looked past him at something he couldn't see.

"Oh my goodness, Joe!" she said. "It's…it's…Mr. Brown was right. It's so beautiful."

She had a look of utter wonder and Joe knew her time here was complete.

"Oh wow! My grandma and….my dog Max is here!" she said, as she hugged someone and then bent down to pet a dog that he couldn't see.

"This is amazing, Grandma," she said, speaking to the air. She started to glow, and then said, "Ok, sounds great! I will be right there!"

As she glowed more brightly, she turned back toward Joe and wrapped her arms around him again. She kissed him on the cheek whispered into his ear, "Thank you for everything."

He hugged back tightly, not wanting to let go. He closed his eyes as the glow emanating from her started to blind him. She felt warmer—almost hot—but it didn't hurt or burn. The glow through his eyelids got brighter and brighter. He whispered back, "I'll never forget you…I lo…" but then trailed off, because as he was about to finish what he intended to say, the glow quickly intensified so much that his eyes hurt, although closed. He felt her body disappear within his embrace. She was no longer there. She was gone.

He couldn't believe what had just happened. The feeling of loss was unbearable. When their friendship began, it all seemed surreal, but was even more so, now that it was over. His friend was gone. He knew he would be forever changed from this experience.

"I'll never forget you," he whispered.

Epilogue

She was gone. Later that night, he found a letter that Mary left for him. When he discovered it under his pillow while going to bed, he jumped up to read it. She must have known her time was short, when they returned home earlier. She had immediately headed to his room so she could write it. He read it eagerly, with tears in his eyes.

Joe,

Well, I guess you found my letter. Hee hee! Unless of course someone else found it first, in which case this letter would seem really weird. But I doubt it; I left it so only you would find it. ☺ *Anyway, I just wanted to take a moment to write you and thank you so much for all you did to help me. I know you were kind of forced into it...I was haunting you after all. But seriously, the past few days were really special for me and I wanted you to know that. You are a special guy. I know you kind of developed feelings for me...I mean, it was pretty obvious.* ☺ *But I kinda developed feelings for you too, so I guess we are even. I know this doesn't make this any easier, though. I wish things could have been different.*

You are going to live a full life and you are going to forget all about me. I just want you to know that it's okay. You are going to have many adventures and meet new people. And when it's time, I'll be waiting for you to tell me all about it. Love you.

Your friend,

Mary

It took a few months for Joe to get back to normal (whatever that was). The rest of the summer, he tried to play it off when he was with his friends but his mind always drifted back to Mary. In time, and especially as the years went past, he thought of her less and less. Life does go on, but one thing was for sure, she was never forgotten.

Joe would always remember his childhood friend and first crush for as long as he lived, and then some.

Joe smiled at the memories as he carefully refolded the letter and gently placed it back into the box. He then put the shoebox back on the top shelf, and as usual, whenever he was finished reading the letter, he'd whisper, just in case it could be heard, "Wherever you are, I hope you are well."

He saw the baseball glove, reminding him why he was in the closet in the first place, and picked it up.

He then headed out of the room, leaving the shoebox and the letter behind on the top shelf.

About the Author

J.E. Jack can be found reading everything from historical textbooks to young adult mystery/thrillers. Developing a love for adventure and self-learning early in life, Joshua has traveled the world and been fortunate enough to survive. With almost two decades of involvement in the military/law enforcement community, he tries to bring different experiences, emotions, and thoughts to his readers. Them Bones is his first novel and is currently writing his second novel. He currently lives near the coast of Louisiana with his family.

If you enjoyed the book and want to see future books by this author, be sure to join us on Facebook by going here: www.facebook.com/authorjejack or by going to the website https://www.jejack.com

Or shoot me an email at authorjejack@gmail.com

Review the Book

You've read my book. Thank you! I truly hope you have enjoyed it. Your feedback is really important to me so if you have a moment, I'd like to ask for you to leave a review. It would be greatly appreciated.

Made in United States
North Haven, CT
29 October 2022

26075580R00136